The Land of Mist

is the second in the authentic and violent
series of the savage days of the Roman
Empire – *The Eagles*

The Land of Mist

Andrew Quiller

Mayflower

Granada Publishing Limited
First published in 1976 by Mayflower Books Ltd
Frogmore, St Albans, Herts AL2 2NF

A Mayflower Original
Copyright © Andrew Quiller 1975
Made and printed in Great Britain by
Cox & Wyman Ltd, London, Reading and Fakenham
Set in Intertype Plantin

This if for Lionel. He has been both lares and penates.
With every good wish.

ONE

Outside Volusia's brothel, The Virgin and the Donkey, the newly risen sun shone smokily down upon the streets and alleys of Rome where the slaves trotted about their masters' business, sleepy vendors took down their shutters and the last country carts were leaving to keep the city free from the grind of iron-rimmed wheels – and, in an upper room of The Virgin and the Donkey, Hierax, the renowned charioteer for the Reds, writhed in mortal agony, very messily choking out his life.

Hierax did not die easily. His breathing burst in ragged gasps of effort, and with increasing difficulty he vomited out a dark green fluid. The two men sitting impassively watching him waited until the green vomit changed to the more sinister hue of blood as Hierax brought up his guts in agonized retchings.

The charioteer's dark curls clustered thickly about his head, sweat soaked, and the cold sweat slicked his face into the spectral likeness of a statue left to rot among the tombs along the Appian Way. His fists gripped and convulsed and his whole body shuddered with the effort of dying.

'Death is certain now, Martialis,' said the taller of the two, sitting there so quietly watching a man die in agony.

'He was a great charioteer and now he has run his last race,' said Martialis, in the gruff arena-voice of the professional gladiator.

'The action of the poison is always fascinating.' The taller man glanced at the clepsydra and marked the level of water. 'I think the denarius is mine. He will be gone before the time of the wager.'

'Your experience should have warned me, as Venus is my witness,' grumbled the gladiator. His squat neck, thick and columnar, carried his small round head poised, always alert, confident. The massive muscles of his body, hardened from wearing the cuirass, rolled as he clenched his fist, about to bring that iron-hard weapon down in a hammerblow upon the table.

'Hold, Martialis! The drabs may sleep; but I'll warrant the old crone Volusia is awake yet, and listening for us.'

'Aye, Pulcher.' Martialis reached for his arm purse and drew forth four sestertii. 'Here is the wager. But I will hold it in my hand until Hierax is gone.'

The charioteer, as though his name called forth the high sound of the trumpets, the horses snorting and stamping their polished hooves in the stalls, the quadriga alive and vibrant with readiness and life, surged upright. A bright stream of scarlet burst from his mouth. He tried to speak, and gargled on his own life's blood, and so, straining every sinew, the charioteer Hierax died.

'Here, Pulcher,' growled Martialis, and threw the coins upon the table. They spun and glittered in the morning light through the high unbarred window which drowned the vague orange glow from the guttering lamp.

Pulcher laughed quietly and took up the coins.

'Experience is a hard-won thing, by the Names. And this fool learned nothing. Had he listened, he would be alive now.'

'Aye.' Martialis rose and drew his cloak about the fanciful tunic he wore, a garment perfectly suited to the grandiose position among the gladiators he occupied. 'But I can understand his reluctance to throw a race. He wished always to win.'

Pulcher, too, rose. His clothes were dark and inconspicuous. The dagger at his waist was lost among folds of cloth, yet the bone handle thrust forward at an angle very ready for an instant draw. 'He wanted to win – and yet he has lost the greatest race of all.'

'And the drab?'

Both men looked at the naked woman sprawled across the settle against the wall beneath the window. Her blood had dripped from her slit throat all the time Hierax had been dying. The pool widened on the floor, dark, creeping, malign.

'Take her up and wrap her in the blanket. Father Tiber may feast upon what is left of her charms.'

Grumbling, Martialis obeyed. 'The factions are hard taskmasters,' he said, tucking the blanket around the limp white form. One plump breast lolled free, the nipple painted coral, and he thrust it back with the careless push of a man stowing cabbages in a sack. 'Now it will be the turn of Vulpus to listen.'

'Vulpus!' said Pulcher. The fingers of his left hand brushed his dagger hilt. 'If he does not win today even *his* renown will not save him.'

8

Martialis grunted and heaved the corpse over his shoulder as though it were a sack of feathers.

'He is a strange man. I would fain fight him for the joy of it; yet I know the ending of that fight only too well.'

'Perhaps he has tired of fighting. As a charioteer he will—'

'No.' The gladiator shook his head, his broken nose turning pugnaciously and his small dark eyes raking Pulcher. 'No. A man like that never tires of fighting. He drives in the races because they offer him a fresh challenge.'

'A challenge he had best meet!'

'Oh, aye. The circus is not like the amphitheatre. He will find that out. The master, the great Clodius Maximus, will soon bring him to heel.'

The thought seemed to give both men pleasure.

They did not bother to blow out the lamp. Its tiny orange flame, blowing this way and that, guttering, brought faint vague shadows flittering about that room of death as the two men left, the body of the drab carried with them, to be thrown by slaves into the Tiber after dark. But, before that would happen, the day's races would have been driven, the Circus Maximus would echo to the shrieks of the multitudes, and men would know, in their turn, who was to live and who to die.

Poppaea, the wife of Helvius Geminus, wore a flaring red scarf which she tore from her neck and waved in wild abandon as the chariots flew past below. All about her on the ranked terraces the riot of colours waved and fluttered and thousands upon thousands of throats bellowed in insane fanaticism the colours of the factions, the names of the charioteers, the names of their near-side horses.

'Pertinax!'

'Green! Green!'

'Blue! Blue!'

'Bucephalus!'

'White! White!'

'Tetius!'

The four chariots whirled along, the disturbed dust smoking into the air after them despite its liberal sprinkling before every race. The sun beat down and there was no velarium here, down at the far end of the course. Poppaea felt that familiar languorous warmth creeping over her. This seat, almost at the second mark, almost opposite the dangerous bend, might not rival those seats set athwart the course and thus affording the best view. But it did give a fine opportunity to view the best smash-ups.

How she longed to see a really good smash today!

Helvius, her stodge of a husband, had sniffed when she had put on the great red scarf.

'Vulpus, I suppose?'

She had ignored him. All he could think of were his wretched business worries, for his cloth merchantry whilst it prospered kept him endlessly at the factory.

He would probably like to forbid her going to the Circus; but was she not a free-born Roman lady? Did she not wear a hem of purple to prove her purity? And was not that purple purity safe from anything that might happen in the Circus?

The chariots had whirled past and now Poppaea could take a fresh interest in the youth who had boldly sat down next to her. She eyed him from the corner of one eye. The law said no one was supposed to bring refreshment into the Circus, and everyone did, so Poppaea munched a date, spitting out the stone with a plop.

'Would you do me the kindness, dear my lady, to favour me with a date?' The youth looked at her artlessly. He was dressed in the height of fashion, his hair curled, his tunic of perfect cut and material, his manner open and winning. 'I think Mars has smitten me, for I melt in the heat.'

Poppaea handed the little basket with the damp moss to him.

'Mars, citizen?' she said. She spoke coyly.

The roar running along the banked seats brought all attention to the track again. This was the third lap. The chariots came into sight, and Poppaea waved her scarf; but this time she was more aware of the youth, whose red favours proclaimed him of the same faction.

The leading quadriga hugged the rail, running swiftly along by the spina, the central island with its monuments and gardens and images of the gods. The leader was the Green.

Hard on his outside and straining to pass, the red chariot hurtled along, the four horses extended, the charioteer plying his whip, the dust pounding from their hooves.

'Red! Red!' shrieked Poppaea.

'Blue! Blue!' a bull-voice bellowed in her ear. The man at her back, red-faced, sweaty, pounded on his seat.

The chariots roared by. As they rounded the bend and fled past so all heads turned to follow them. Poppaea squealed.

'Pertinax! He gains on the thrice-accursed Green!'

'I am sure he does – see – they go into the far bend neck and neck!'

'Your Pertinax is an idiot!' declared the fat man, red-faced, sure of himself. 'He takes the bend outside of the Green! He wastes his four's strength. Blue hugs the rail and will come from the back on the last straight! You will see!'

The bedlam continued as the quadrigas rounded the course again and the next ball and dolphin were removed from the marks at each end of the spina. The fourth and fifth laps saw no change in the situation. But the youth stood now very close to Poppaea. On the sixth lap she leaned towards him and his arm went around her waist. The sun beat down, the dust rose, the multitude, all two hundred and fifty thousand of them, bellowed and roared and stamped. No one could hear any individual voice.

On the last lap White shot past Blue in an attempt to rake in before the bend. The iron-rimmed wheels spurted dust.

'Look out! Pertinax!' screamed Poppaea – screamed thousands of those sporting the red colour.

The wall of sound battered the senses. The heat stifled. White's inside horse, his master horse on trace only, clipped the rear of Red's chariot. The car swerved. Holding on to the reins with his left hand, their remaining length wound about his waist, Pertinax in his red tunic flogged on his horses.

But his car had been skewed off course. Poppaea felt faint with excitement. She was aware of the track, of the pounding horses, of the pounding of her heart in unison, of the youth's hand slipping up her waist to cup her breast, of the chariots bounding, of fingers and thumb probing her nipple, of Red's car turning over – of the flash of a knife as the reins were cut. The horses bolted into the last straight, the car dragged into smashed ruin behind them. A hand was at her knee, her thigh, was probing. She was wet through and through. The charioteer's head squashed like a pumpkin under the rim of White's wheel. Poppaea screamed and squirmed and moved herself wantonly against the youth, reaching for him, gripping him, making him gasp.

The bright blood splashed across the sand below.

Then the chariots were flashing past the line and the crowd

were yelling or shrieking and the bets were being paid off and the young man was drawing back and looking at her with a slight smile. Her face was as red as the spilt blood. She felt engorged.

'What a smash!' she said.

The youth indicated the seat and sat down, crossing his legs. 'I pray the next may be even better,' he said, smiling.

'Oh, yes! For – Vulpus is to drive!'

'Vulpus, the gladiator! Vulpus, the Fox!'

The chariot gleamed.

Sunlight fell through gratings above the stall, throwing dramatic shadows into the corners where the scores of handlers and stable boys and sprinklers and attendants busied themselves each to his allotted task – but, in the centre, the chariot gleamed.

Old Tacho, grey-haired and bent, his tunic already smeared with grease, laboured with cunning skill to work his grease into the inmost part of the axles, making sure both wheels ran with a sure sweet freedom. The old conditore would never taste freedom; born a slave, he would grease wheels as a conditore until he could grease no longer. After that, given that his master, the notorious Clodius Maximus had no further use for him, he might be turned off, sold with a parchment scroll at his neck, even quietly butchered and disposed of, as being the easiest and cheapest way of getting rid of a worn-out slave.

A sparsore with his cleaning-rags working busily to make the chariot gleam the brighter, spat and rubbed, his young muscles lithe. Well, one day he, the feckless young slave Sanum, would be an old and worn-out sparsore, and his cleaning days would be over.

The stall resounded with its own peculiar noises, of clicking and clacking, the hiss and spit of men at work, the clatter of buckets. Above those small noises the sounds of the horses came surprisingly muted. The four animals gleamed so gloriously in the falling sunlight that the eyes crinkled to watch. And, over all the noises, the immense uproar from the stadium burst through the closed stall doors like, as Marcus thought every time, like the sea waves smashing and breaking whitely against the rocks of Britain's shore.

The armentarii handled their charges with the care that resulted from the dread knowledge that the horse was worth a hundred slaves like them, that a single hair of its head, a hair of its mane or tail was more precious than their miserable skins. The grooms worked, like everyone else here, at last-minute preparations before the stall gates opened and the chariots shot out into the sunshine and the plaudits and the fierce and un-yielding competition along the sand.

Special sand, too. None of your common stuff was good enough for the stadium of the Circus Maximus, the oldest and greatest of the stadia in Rome.

Marcus pulled his red tunic straight and inspected the whips a slave brought to him. Over in the shadows men wearing togas came forward, grave-faced men in the normal way; but now they were men whose faces showed the passionate absorption with horses and chariots, a driving force of their lives, far greater in importance than stuffy senate business that meant nothing now that Domitian controlled all. These men, these patricians – aye! and these freedmen with enormous wealth, jumped-up nouveau-riches – these fanatics of the hippodrome knew every trick in the tablets.

That was the only good thing Marcus had ever heard said about the Dominus, about the owner, about Clodius Maximus.

The man loved horses.

In a scoundrel as black as an Ethiop's arse, that was a re-deeming feature. The only one.

The heat made everyone sweat, and Clodius fussily de-manded that the shutters be opened wider to admit more air.

Slaves sprang to do his bidding.

Those with him fawned. Well, the professional parasites could do that job superbly well; some of the others with Clodius made Marcus's lip curl in contempt. But he had no business with them. He drove this quadriga, the four horses he knew personally and well; the chariot was a superb specimen, and he knew his own skill. No, he had no business with Clodius or his clique apart from driving. As far as he knew they had had no hand in the disgrace of his father, legate of the XX Legio, that great man who had taken the honourable Roman way out of disgrace in suicide.

'Vulpus!' Clodius waddled forward, not so much grossly fat for a short man but obscenely unpleasant in girth, all soft wobble within the tunic and toga. His oiled and perfumed body must resemble a pig's bladder of blood, squashable, whitely

smooth, gurgling. His face showed all the fashionable minis-
trations: plucked hair, painted cheeks, painted lips, sooted eyebrows. His jewellery glittered like the eternal fires over the
Vesuvius.

'Clodius,' said Marcus, as a citizen of Rome accorded that
privilege. Marcus Julius Britannicus, son of a Roman noble and
a Princess of the Icenii, the Princess Elfleda. Well, they were
both dead, and Marcus could look back at the blood trail and
see where it washed clean and where the black marks of treachery remained.

'Reds need a win today, my Vulpus!'

'The quadriga is as fine as any I have seen. But I am told the
Greens have Eutychus driving for them—'

'Eutychus!' burst out Clodius, all his chins gobbling. 'The
man may have five hundred and seventy wins, but he can be
beaten.'

'Five hundred and eighty-one, Dominus,' said Nonius, the
parasite, a thin man with the expectant expression of a sparrow
continually on the look-out for crumbs. He waved a ringed
hand negligently. 'Yes, my Clodius. This Eutychus is a worthy
match.'

'And this Vulpus of yours,' said Flavius Longus, in his harsh
legionary's bark, 'has but ten victories.'

Marcus looked at the patrician with interest, wondering what
a man who was so obviously not long from the ranks of the
Legions could be doing in the company of men like Clodius and
Nonius and the others of this clique. The soldier wore a red
favour on his civilian clothes. Maybe it was purely the passion
for the Circus.

'That is true, Flavius,' said Marcus in his own harsh way, not
caring to dissemble. 'I have but ten victories.' He paused as the
soldier glared in surprise. Then he added in a quiet voice: 'And
I have driven but ten races.'

'Now, by Mithras! This I do not believe!'

Flavius looked at Marcus as he spoke, and something in
Marcus's iron-hard face checked him. He half-lifted a hand.
The mad glare in Marcus's brown eyes gave the soldier an
abrupt sensation of an icy feather passing down his spine. He
swallowed. Marcus stared at him, waiting.

'Mayhap I spoke over-hastily.' Flavius Longus licked his
lips. 'By Mithras! You would be a man for the first cohort of
any legion!'

Marcus did not laugh, although that would have been a good and possibly expected reaction. Instead, as the images of Masada, of the western mountains, of deserts, rose in his mind, blurred with the red flicker of weapons, he turned away and took the whip he had selected.

He cracked the lash down and jerked his arm up, and the flat smash as the whip flicked through the air underlined all that was not said.

Truth to tell, Mithras had more than smiled on him since he had consented to drive for Clodius. He had been lucky. By the Names! He had driven ten times, and each time, by a fluke, by luck, by a madness in his driving that recked nothing of consequences, he had passed the winning-line first. That could not go on, of course. Everyone knew that of the four factions the Blues and the Greens were the strongest. The Whites and the Reds were the second runners. The emperor, this Domitian of whom Marcus and many more harboured deep suspicions after the reigns of his brother Titus and his father Vespasian, was like to extend the factions. Well, what might come of that no one could say, as no one could say quite how Domitian would conduct himself. There were already dark stories current.

The blare of trumpets and the noise of the crowd heralded the cessation of the interval. Somewhere out on the sands the procuratores dromi would be smoothing down the ridges and the scurf marks, covering the puddles of blood – there was always blood, thick and greasy, to provide enjoyment for the crowd. Old wine-skins, gnawed bones, half-eaten cakes, chewed scraps of meat, all were tossed madly into the air as the races went on, and all must be cleared away, the sand raked and sprinkled and made ready for the next race. In Augustus Caesar's time there had been twelve races each day; now there were twenty-four and this talk was of Domitian not only increasing the number of colours but also the number of races. Well, all that remained to be seen.

'Are you ready, master?'

Vulpus nodded.

Old Diocles knew most of the tricks of racing. He'd already chalked up three hundred or more wins when an unlucky fall had smashed up his arm. Now he was one of the most valued of slaves to have at one's side, teaching, cursing, domineering; but always with the dread knowledge of a flogging in his heart to keep him in order. Vulpus coiled the whip around his right arm, for he would not need that yet. He walked towards his car.

His funalis, his left-hand horse, curved his glossy neck as Marcus approached.

'Well, my Zephyr! And will you run true for me today?'

The horse, a magnificent black, as were the four, blew again, snorting, revealing a nostril redder than the reddest rose. Marcus stroked him with genuine emotion. On him, on this funalis, Zephyr, rested his true fortunes. Oh, he was not like old Pluto, that massive warhorse, a midnight black, given to him by his father. Pluto was a waler with mouth of iron, hooves of iron, thews of iron, and a heart of purest gold burnished in the fires of Hades. Pluto would carry him into the domains for which his god-name called; but Zephyr! Ah, Zephyr could run so close to the rail of the spina and clip precious moments off the turn, and yet judge to a sweet nicety the distance so that the snarling iron lion-boss of the chariot axle should not foul the granite of the three metae marking the end. Looking like cypress trees, and supposed to act as bumpers, the metae would smash a chariot to kindling in a twinkling.

Yes, Zephyr was a horse for the gods.

And the right-hand horse, Endymion, also running only on a trace as the left-hand horse; he, too, was a matchless steed with a heart that would run until it burst. His job came on the turns where he must wheel around outside and drag the chariot with him in alignment, neither pressing too hard on the inner horses nor running wide and so dragging them to a reduction of speed. These two tracers were the two most important horses in the team.

But -- there were Impiter and Gladius, the two yokers, to give the hauling power, to run and run and think of nothing else but running. Both these two black beauties were fine horses, part of a team. Gladius, named for the short, straight, stabbing sword of the Legions that had won an Empire, would do all that his name suggested. Like the gladius in a legionary's hand he would dart straight ahead, undeviating, powerful, a massive thrusting force. Then it was up to Endymion on his right to edge him around the corners, and for the master horse, Zephyr, to control the amount of turn so as to bring the axle-boss humming past the granite of the metae a hand's breadth away, sweet and true.

Seven laps of the course, there were. Seven balls and seven dolphins. Thirteen turns. And every heart-beat a moment for disaster and destruction.

And, of all those heart-beats of destruction, perhaps the most fearsome was the moment of beginning, when the white cloth fell and the trumpets sounded and the stall doors flew open on their ropes and the four quadrigas flashed forward for the starting line. Here was the time for experience and for boldness, for cunning and courage.

The course ran left-handed, and the central spina was slightly angled so as to make the entrance on to the first straight narrow imperceptibly, like a funnel. From the metae at the end of the spina across to the stands was stretched a white rope, hoof-high. If the start was not correct, if carnage occurred early, as it so often did, the judge would not call for the rope to be dropped. The race would not be officially started. Of course, if a plunging team crashed into the rope, that was the fault of the charioteer.

Marcus Julius Britannicus had learned about that Mithras-forsaken rope from Diocles.

'You go hell-for-leather for the rope, Vulpus, and you're wearing the good old Red, and the judge is a secret supporter of the Greens, may the gods strike their guts with the dropping-sickness, he'll not drop the rope on a pretext. Anything will do – after you're splashed all over the sand.'

Marcus had nodded. He understood this kind of stratagem. He had learned in the arena, he had learned the gladiatorial tricks from his old instructor, back in Britain, from old Argos. Now he listened to Diocles, remembering his days driving the British chariots, where he had picked up a skill not understood by these Roman charioteers. But he listened. He was not called Vulpus the Fox for nothing.

'Aye, Vulpus. You may slip your gladius as sweetly as any man into the guts of a retiarius who's lost his net and who's trident is broken. But in the Circus it's different.' Diocles had shifted his ruined arm, his eyes faded and yet still giving a memory of the decision in split-seconds they held. 'And the same fat-bellied whoreson who secretly supports the Greens holds the rope up to trip the horses – and you haul back, cannily, like I've taught you – and Green, who knows! Who knows, the bastard! He knows he can go full speed at the rope and his friend will drop it at the very last moment as the first horse's hoof lifts to smash into it! Aye, Vulpus! It's all dirty tricks, here in the Circus!'

'And blood and death just as surely.'

The mounted agitatores each to their colour would be ready to assist their chariots. The crowd yells had muted, save for the occasional baying of a section, led by their leaders, chanting the colour, the funalis or the charioteer of their faction.

The crowd out there were waiting.

Leaving his four, with a final pat and endearment for each, Marcus walked back to his car. He mounted slowly and carefully, he did not spring with an abandoned leap into the car. For one thing, the whole contraption was so skimpy that an incautious boot would go straight through. He braced his feet, diagonally across the floor, and his assistants selected out the reins, passed from the ring at the end of the shaft, through the rings on the inside of each horse's bit, and so back to him. There were yards of rein. He took each one carefully, shaking it, getting the feel of it. Then with the help of the aurigatores he passed the ends of the reins around and around his body. This was important. By leaning back on the ribbons he would haul up the team. They supported him, in conjunction with the special charioteer's stance. As he did this so Marcus put a hand, quite instinctively, down to the knife scabbarded at his waist. He would not care to lose that knife. No charioteer would. They patronized Venus, and they'd be praying hard to her; well, Marcus had been a son of the Legion; Mithras was for him.

The Circus Maximus, crowded by the buildings of Rome, had grown up in the valley of Murcia. A tiny stream had flowed down the centre of the valley – now that stream was a mere drain running under the spina. The valley had been clustered with myrtle – and myrtle was sacred to Venus. So the charioteers, like everyone else, confounded the goddess Murcia with Venus, and prayed to the divine goddess of the place for victory.

The group with Clodius gave their last-minute expressions of good will, calling usually on a plethora of gods so as to be on the safe side. Marcus, known as Vulpus, stood watching them, the reins about his waist gathered into his left hand and his right merely hanging limp, the whip coiled.

Clodius Maximus waddled across, waving away the slaves still fussing over the equipage. The noise from outside drove in, muted, menacing, *hungry.*

Clodius tilted up his head so that his chins stretched into a shining globular mass. His beringed hand hooked on to the brass rim of the chariot.

'Vulpus!'

Marcus inclined his head.

Clodius spoke in a voice pitched so as to reach Marcus and no one else. That voice, so hoarse, so breathy, so pig-like in its grunting snort, sickened Marcus. And yet – and yet! What the whoreson said made Marcus more than sick – so much more that he did not move a muscle of his face, remained stock still, his face as iron-hard and unyielding as ever.

'Vulpus,' said this Clodius Maximus, this great noble, this fanatic of the Reds. 'I command you not to win this race. I believe you can, if Venus smiles upon you. But you will not win. You may shipwreck, or, if that is not to your taste, you may hold and finish. But you will not win!'

As Marcus said nothing and did not move, Clodius rapped a gemmed knuckle upon the brass of the chariot.

'Do you hear me, you stiff-necked bastard?'

Marcus looked down at him.

'I hear you.'

'Then remember what you have been told.' A strange, toad-like look came over Clodius's face. 'You were a friend to Hierax, I believe?'

Marcus felt the brilliant anger in him, that had been controlled, contained, a thing to be used, turn instantly to ice. Hierax – everyone had been talking of it all morning.

'So Hierax had the courage—' he began.

'Not so! Hierax was a fool. I do not think you are a fool, Vulpus.'

'And you are of the Reds! What of the familia quadrigaria! What of your pride, Clodius!'

The equestrian's face flushed with blood. His eyes almost vanished in the pudgy rolls of fat. He lifted his hand as though to summon his personal bodyguard to cut down this charioteer. There were jubilatories and there were jubilatories. There were gladiators and there were gladiators. He had heard so much of this Vulpus, this fighting machine men called Vulpus the Fox. The man was no slave. There clung about him the romantic aura of the patrician, the man who might be mocked and condemned, laughed at, for daring to fight in the arena or race in the stadium; but, indisputably, this Vulpus was dangerous. He would have to be treated carefully, far more carefully than Hierax.

'I tell you now, Vulpus, for your own good and for the last time. I did not tell you before. I tell you now. I do not wish you to win—'

A trumpet sounded.

Marcus, Vulpus the Fox, held back as his horses surged impatiently forward, snorting, pawing the ground, blowing.

The slaves whose responsibility it was to get the equipage clear, all of them with their different roles, were clearly growing frightened. If the master did not leave soon, there would be a disaster.

'I hear you, Clodius. I do not yet know what to do—'

'You'll lose, Vulpus, you'll lose, or you'll be deader than Hierax!'

'What a glorious smash-up that was!' said Poppaea, sitting and regarding the youth. 'Oh, how I hope there is another, even more glorious! But not to Vulpus!' she added, quickly, her breath catching. 'Oh, not to Vulpus!'

The youth smiled his simpering smile and sat, and unfolded his tablets. The score card showed the next race under the various usual headings: Faction: Team: Horse colour: Driver: Stall. Poppaea fumbled about her plump person for her own tablets, contriving to drop her basket of dates. The young man quickly picked them up for her, blowing on two that had rolled in the dust.

Poppaea thanked him dutifully.

The score card showed that Reds had been allotted stall three. The young man frowned. He shook his head.

'Greens have carcer one, and Whites carcer two. Blues have carcer four. It is not a good draw, not a good draw.'

'But Vulpus has never lost—'

'There is always the first time. Ten wins out of ten races. By the Names! He must be beloved by Venus. Mayhap she has come down to him in the guise of a horse, and shows him all he needs as they run.'

Poppaea busied herself with her tablets. She had shouted her bets to the touts running up and down the aisles, and if Helvius scolded her she'd pour out her winnings. Vulpus always won. The odds were poor against him; but the presence in this race of Eutychus, a champion for the Greens, had given a lift to the betting.

'Yes, Eutychus will give Vulpus a hard race.'

'And what of Eusebius?' bellowed the fat man from the seat to their rear, the man who supported the Blues. 'By Jupiter the Best and Greatest! Is not Eusebius's Pollux the best funalis in all Rome? A double centenarius?'

'I'll grant you, sir, that Pollux has won over a hundred races, and is therefore a centenarius. But two hundred?'

The fat man laughed until tears ran from his eyes. He slapped his fat thighs. 'One hundred and ninety and nine times has Pollux won, and so today, I deem him already a centenarius.'

'Presumption!' said Poppaea, in her best and most cultivated cutting of ways. It never failed to subdue those of her friends who presumed too much.

'Beware, lady,' called the Blues supporter, 'that Vulpus's family – if he have a family – do not carry a coin to the Temple of Libitina.'

Poppaea felt so outraged she shuddered. Her upper lip was quite damp. She looked at the young man, whose name, he had said, was Fabius.

This Fabius remembered the succulent moist warmth of the lady whose name he had not yet had the delicacy to inquire. Plump she might be; the easy wife of a husband to be cuckolded she most certainly was, and one who would be generous with her gifts. He would probably please her greatly. Ah! Bless Venus the day the Games were first created, and the Circus, great above all! Why, when he went to watch those great huge sweaty gladiators hacking each other to pieces, he had to sit among men, and he wasn't like his pallid friend Cleanthe, who was more Greek than Roman. But at the Circus! Ah, there men and women sat where they liked, and many a knee was stroked, many a thigh caressed and a plump white breast massaged as the iron-rimmed chariot wheels scythed the dust and the people screamed themselves red in the face. And – red! This fellow of the Blues – if he was allowed to be too domineering then the fat little lady at his side, who offered so much, would turn away to that gaunt quill-scratcher on her other side, whose fingers had had to be beaten away from the lady's thighs the previous race.

Fabius leaned back, all a negligent arrogant pose of a fashionable Roman youth, one of the bloods. Everyone here knew their place. There was no pretence that any were of the quality to occupy the podium at the patrician and equestrian end of the stadium. He leaned back on an elbow and said: 'I had assumed, my friend, that Libitina was your patron, and you were, in truth, yourself a libitinari.'

Poppaea felt pleased. Neat ... Calling the upstart Blue fellow an undertaker, a caterer for the dead, was nice.

Blue started to his feet, his face betraying allegiance to quite another colour, and a trumpet shrilled and after a single golden instant of silence the stands erupted.

The yells broke down to the usual four colours, and to the names of Eutychus, Gallicus, Eusebius, Vulpus, the charioteers, the men who were risking their necks out there. And, also, the name of each funalis: Thessalus, Victor, Pollux, Zephyr, the left-hand horses that would control and dominate and design the race – if they were given the chance.

The tension that had built up during the day increased now as the multitude – what they called the cavea in the slang – waited for this race. The importance of any race varied with many factors; the Games went on for a large number of days a year, with chariot racing a part of the greater whole. What the particular celebration was, Poppaea was unaware, and was not particularly mindful, unless it was her own patroness – all was subdued to the intense excitement of the here and now.

All Poppaea cared about was that her idol, Vulpus, Vulpus the Fox, was ready to drive out, and race against death – and as she waved her red scarf she knew with all the secret passion of her body, that Vulpus was racing for her!

A scatter of slaves still struggled to clear and smooth the course. Although obstructed much in her view by the central spina with its obelisks and gardens and altars, the one to Consus giving a thin line of incense smoke to the sky, she could see the scurry of activity opposite the other end of the spina. It was a trifle difficult to make out what was happening and the crowd began to grow noisy above their usual baying for colour, horse or driver. The multitude grew more and more restless, wroth that this delay should baulk them of pleasure.

More trumpets sounded.

Slaves scurried and ran – but then the beast howl as a quarter of a million throats bellowed: 'They're off!' signalled as nothing else could that the race had begun.

The four stall doors flew open at the tug of ropes, the four chariots shot forth like giant darts from giant ballistae. Their wheels scarcely touching the sand, the hooves of the horses seeming to spurn the track, they belted for the white rope hanging just above the ground.

Outside, Blue gave a reckless lash with his whip, early in the race – early!

Blue's chariot fled for the line. If he could do it – if he could reach it and seize the inside . . .

The shrieks were not of warning, or of fear, or of pity.

The shrieks were of excitement and of intense physical pleasure so soon gratified.

The procuratores dromi bundled to the side, out of the way. The last to run was too late.

He was a middle-aged slave, exhausted of face, thin of limb, with that betraying reddish-pink about his eyes which told he suffered from conjunctivitis, the pink-eye so common among the workers among dust and smoke, a common complaint in Imperial Rome.

He stared up, horrified.

His mouth was wide open and his neck strained. He was screaming at the top of his voice; nothing could be heard save the solid waves of sound belching from the cavea. He threw an ineffectual hand to his head. He went over backwards, his dusty tunic abruptly burst with a torrent of blood as the kicking hooves trampled drummingly down upon him. He was kicked and flung a dozen yards, spraying blood, cartwheeling over and over, one arm, severed by a razor-sharp battering of hooves, spinning off and splattering those in the lowest tier of seats.

The wheels missed him. That made no difference to him; it probably saved Eusebius from complete catastrophe. Blue's funalis staggered for three paces only; then Pollux gathered himself, a superb centenarius, gathered himself and recovered and was bursting to get into the position he knew he must be in for the race. But that single slave had thrown Blue back.

Poppaea saw.

She screamed and a stream of liquid ran down her thigh, warm and wet and somehow infinitely comforting.

'See!' she screamed. 'See! Your stinking Blue Pollux is back, is back! Vulpus! Vulpus kicks dust in his face!'

No one heard her, of course.

The four chariots screamed for the line.

Clodius Maximus had gone back to his perfumed seat among the nobles. The handlers could make their last-minute final adjustments. The atmosphere of tension, of swift sweaty activity, of professional expertise extended to the utmost, of quick nervous sensitivity from the pared readiness of the horses to the final smoothing of a buckle, the flick of a duster to a wheel spoke, all contributed to the sudden dry-mouthed sense that the world waited to jerk into motion.

Up there, over his head, Clodius would be settling into his silken seat, cushioned and comfortable, and his cronies would be fawning and the bets being passed in imitation negligent patrician drawls. Domitian, of course, in his royal box, had the best of all views. Marcus surmised sourly that Clodius was working towards the ear of the emperor. Well, much good that would do him.

Throw the race!

Deliberately to go out there and lose!

Marcus had lost all fine ideals and noble ideas of honour and glory, except where the honour of his family touched him dearly. Despite what the Romans had done to his family and to his great aunt, who, for some reason, they called Boadicea, he had been brought up to revere Rome and her institutions, to see that the empire was a reality, and that it held the lamp of civilization burning in the streaming barbarian winds.

Oh, no, honour would demand he toss Clodius's orders aside as beneath the contempt of a patrician.

Self-interest told him that he'd be a dead man if he did.

Common sense told him to wait and see what fortune the race itself brought.

The doctore, old Diocles, made his last adjustments, stepped back, his nut-cracker face filled with his envy, and yet with his goodwill. Diocles would have given a deal to be up there, in that chariot, with a good left arm to grasp the reins . . .

'Remember, Vulpus, my brave one! Eutychus has the renown and the experience; but you can take him. It is Eusebius, the Blue, you must watch. If he takes your wheel track, he will take your wheel!'

Marcus nodded. It was old advice, nothing new; but it fitted here. If a charioteer could edge his wheel behind yours and then swing abruptly away he could take your wheel off as cleanly as a tooth pulled by a string tied to a donkey's tail.

But you had to belabour the donkey first, or stick him with a red hot iron. No Mithras-forsaken Blue was going to do that to a Red – nor a Green or White, either . . .

Marcus had not asked how Pertinax had fared in the previous race. No one had volunteered the information. Marcus took a final grip on the reins. Had Pertinax won they'd have come running to tell him, flushed with jubilation. Even second, they'd have told him. Third or last, they might have made some surly remark or two. But nothing at all meant Pertinax would never drive again.

The delay must have at last been ended, for the trumpets shrilled again.

The editor must have dropped his white scarf – yes, with a little betraying initial jerk, a groan and then a sudden rush as of a vulture flapping to take flight, the doors gapped open.

The horses, let slip by their straining attendants, bolted through the doors.

Immediately, the chariot took to its wings.

If those iron-rimmed wheels touched the ground they must do so in enormous bounds. The horses, extended, their heads pointed, their manes all bobbed and glittering with semi-precious stones, with red the predominant colour, seemed to soar through the air. Sunlight smashed down. The noise became impossible. Heat and noise and light, brilliant, confining, condensing. And the chariot bounding glittering after the gleaming forms of the horses, their long legs a blur of muscled power, dust spitting back. A shimmer of white to his left, a vaguer shimmer of blue to his right, and a thing – a bundle of rags – directly in his path!

The rags moved, scuttling, and Marcus with his eyes fixed on the spina and the entrance to the track and the Alba Linea hanging like a drawn sword across the track, caught the vaguest glimpse of movement and rags hurtling, like a straw dummy, and the bright scarlet spray of blood, and a sudden swiftly-vanished stink, and a single scarlet drop spitting across his cheek – and then he was away and Blue swerved into his rear and the spina was hurtling at him and White was pinched and it was Green on the rail and Red on his outside as they poured into the straight, with White on the rail behind with Blue on his outside.

It had been quick, fast, and deadly.

The rope had dropped even as Green's horses reached it.

Marcus cursed. He cursed foully and by the most Druidical

of gods. He could even call down the wrath of Mithras upon the wretch who had so bungled it all for him. Here he was, set up in the most vulnerable position – outside the master Eutychus and trailed by the dark horse, the sinister Blue, Eusebius.

It mattered nothing that somewhere in that enormous multitude a thousand women like Poppaea screamed in joy and relief that their idol Vulpus had successfully bounded ahead of Blue and White. They might wet themselves with glee and released excitement; they knew nothing.

On his left Green hugged the rail and went like a bat out of hell. To his rear Blue trampled on ready to smash his car up at the first opportunity. The whip lay still coiled upon his right arm. The chariots smoked down the track. The first corner approached and the first crisis of the race proper.

Only superb judgment would keep him in the race at all now, only split-second decision and divine driving would keep him alive at all.

Green took the bend with a mastery that told the centenarius, Thessalus, knew exactly what he was doing.

The quadriga went around the bend as though on rails.

Red was seen to take the bend wider, and so dropped back, and wider still on the straight as they fled down the back straight. White bored on in the track of Green. And there was a space between Green and Red, and Blue could come up into it, there was room, Blue could bore through to take the second position from Red.

Marcus cast a rapid glance to his left. The chariot leaped and bucked like a coracle in a wild Silurian stream. Eutychus was leaning back on his reins, holding his four in, his whip coiled, leaning back and laughing as his dark eyes met Marcus's.

Leaning back in his turn, braced by feet and reins, Marcus heard over all the noise the trampling onset of Blue's quadriga behind him. But Blue was a little to his left. Eusebius could not now smash on to his car and wreck him all across the sand unless he pulled over. Well, he could do that if he chose . . .

What happened then came as though those dark and bloody Druidical gods of Old Britain had answered him. Perhaps it was Mithras, after all. Certainly none of the old gods mattered much these days; Neptune, the god of horses, might turn a fishy eye away from his creatures used like this. And Venus, too, despite the offerings to her before the races, might not care overmuch for them. As for Jupiter, Greatest and Best, he was

26

probably hard at work somewhere fathering a new race of giants.

White saw his chance.

He saw the gap opening between Red and Green and with a quick whipping up of his four he edged across, his funalis, Victor, perfectly understanding what was required. The horse probably knew more than the charioteer; Marcus had completely misjudged Gallicus. The charioteer had won a number of times, and had come second and third on many more; he made his move far too early in the race.

Despite that, Gallicus, driving White, no doubt imagining that his highly touted four had the beating of Green's in a straight race, bored for the gap.

Locked in a chequered pattern they barrelled out of the corner and smoked down the straight. Wheels spun in arcs of flashing light. Dust flew from the horses' hooves, trailing a long smear down the track into which the quadrigas plunged again on the next turn around.

Marcus came out of the bend wider still. White whipped-up again. All Marcus had done with his whip so far was to touch the shoulder of his horse lightly, so as to indicate the moment for the best turn. Driving wide, he had to keep Zephyr from closing the rail, as was natural.

White bucketted on, his car leaping as his four leaped.

He eased between Red and Green. Marcus could see the horses' heads, low for pulling and yet high with effort, their nostrils distended, the membranes red with brilliant blood, straining, the eyes staring, bright and fixed. How beautiful were horses seen thus in the midst of galloping! How superbly wonderful a creation!

Just what happened there Marcus did not see.

One moment he was leaning back so as to give White clear room, with Green presumably urging his quadriga on so as to deny White the lead – the next, and White's car had gone all to pieces.

The wheels ran crazily across the track to roll and bound high against the wall. The chariot itself broke into a tumbling shower of gleaming shivers. Splinters of wood that had no meaning showered across the sand.

Gallicus was dragged bodily by the reins about his waist, plucked through the air, hurled to the sand, and drawn in a bounding mass after his horses. The gleam of a knife showed, vanishing at once. Gallicus did not cut himself free. He rolled, writhing with the bonds about his waist, the bonds that chained him to his death.

He rolled, swerving sideways, rolled, no doubt shrieking like the doomed man he was.

His four shot ahead, frightened, freed from the weight of the chariot and yet alarmed by the unaccustomed brevity of their command. The drag infuriated them. They swerved as one, swerved before Marcus who cursed and strained with his whole body and his muscular left arm and hauled his four across to the right, wide.

Blue came pounding through.

Blue pounded on and those iron hooves that had battered the life from a slave battered down the life from a charioteer. Eusebius did not swerve or flinch. He lashed his whip, a master stroke, cutting across the rump of Gallicus's Victor and the horse leaped, screaming.

Wide swerved the White four, driving for the side. Blue barrelled on through, hooves, wheels, all crunching over the rolling entangled body of Gallicus.

The Green and the Blue shot ahead, and Red, on the outside and wide, followed them down the straight and into the far bend.

White's four galloped on, dragging the mangled, blood-spouting lump of flesh and blood that had once been a charioteer.

Marcus had seen accidents like that before, had seen with shocked horror as the wiry Iceni ponies hauled Domnal off to a shattered, crushed, horrifying death. That had been when he had been a child, growing up with half of him with Legio XX and the other half a wild barbarian child with the Iceni. Later he had seen other ways in which chariots could be shattered, he remembered the land of mist, and the wilderness and the barbarity, the peaked snow-clad mountains, the rushing icy streams, the sacred groves of oak and mistletoe. That had been in the sixth year of Vespasian – yes, the sixth – and Marcus had been nineteen, two years older and wiser since the time he had bidden Samuel ben Ezra and his sister Rachel farewell at the foot of the Serpent's Path leading down from doomed Masada. The Rock of Masada. And then, after that, it had been back to Rome and training and pondering his future, and drinking, and vengeance.

Marcus's future had been unsure, then, dark and thorny.

His mind went back . . .

TWO

'By the face and breasts of Helen, my Julius, I swear your gladius has the wizardry of Achilles himself in its metal!'

Marcus smiled, somewhat gently, and withdrew his sword. It nestled against the oiled and silken-white skin of young Pomponius Endor. Had the thrust been intended, had it been a thumbnail to the left, Pomponius Endor would have been retching blood all over the marble floor and his guts would probably be kissing his knees.

'Mayhap, my Pomponius. But do you speak low of metal, here.'

Endor looked about guiltily. He had fancied himself as a swordsman and nothing would satisfy him but he must match blades with this hard and silent youth, this M. Julius Britannicus, who had come so lately from Judaea.

'In Syria,' put in Flavius Martinus, a negligent, florid young man who prospered on his name, being a genuine if distant relative of the emperor. 'In Syria, I am told, the whores all carry a knife to do that to the legionaries they sleep with.'

How easy for Marcus to have said: 'Then I suggest you take a trip there, Flavius Martinus, and discover if what you hear in Rome is true where men fight battles.'

But he had learned much since those days in Masada — those days in which, despite his life-loving outlook he had come to try to understand the Zealots and their dark creed of death, and, failing to do so, had taken comfort from the escape of Samuel ben Ezra and Rachel.

And that last farewell kiss!

Strange, that passionate, hot, tongue-seeking kiss from a silent, withdrawn shy virgin of the Jews!

They were a race of people with whom Marcus felt he had not yet done.

Of one thing he was absolutely certain. Whatever the rights and wrongs of their case, and of what they had done, he knew without reservations that he admired them. He admired them for their strengths and their courage.

Mind you, if the old Tenth were ordered out to burn

Jerusalem again, well, if his duty called him there to do that, he would go and do it. He was, after all, a Roman.

Around them the smallish room off the main palaestra contained only the cronies of this clique of smart young men. Naked blades, real metal gladii, were not permitted. Here the wooden rudis alone should be used. But Pomponius Endor had been so desperately importunate that Marcus had not cared to deny him. After all, the young puppy was going as a military aide with S. Julius Frontinus, a man of deep thoughts, or perhaps a man of cloudy thoughts, the judgment of which would afford Marcus some future amusement, seeing how closely the resolution would touch his own fortunes.

Now Flavius Martinus, with a string of loose and barely comprehensible oaths, declared he was thirsty and was for a wineshop where a man might drink himself silly like any pleb and vomit everything away for the night's more serious pleasures, by Venus's belly and thighs!

Pomponius beckoned his freedman, a thin wisp of a fellow with that certain lined gaunt face that told of many secrets tucked away in the sinewy old heart beating beneath those bony ribs.

'Here, Basilus, take the swords out — carefully wrapped, mind! You will bear the blame if they are discovered.'

'As you say, master,' and Basilus, with a bow, took the two gladii and wrapped them in their oiled cloths and then in a white sheeting and then in a leather bag. This he slung over a scrawny shoulder and went out, slopping along silently on his sandals, his back bent. Marcus stared after him. A man to be watched.

The tall and narrow-opening door had one wooden valve open only and towards this went Basilus. As he reached it he was flung back, twisting, toppling on his old sandals. His arms flew up. He gave a sharp cry, of surprise more than pain, and fell. Marcus, for one, felt a surge of relief as the leather bag hit the marble silently, the padding cloths muffling the blades within.

'Out of my way, you dung-faced whoreson!'

Into the room strode the strong athletic form of a patrician, a youth who knew exactly what life owed him, knew exactly his position in life, and would use the latter to take the former.

Basilus made no further sound. He merely scrabbled himself to his feet, tottered to the leather bag and so, silently, stumbled out. Marcus had seen the bloody nose where the newcomer's fist had caught him.

'Your freedman, was it, Caius?'

Caius Pomponius Endor nodded.

'Yes, Gnaeus.'

'I've no time to waste. His excellency the governor—' This arrogant Gnaeus caught himself. 'I mean Q. Petillius Cerialis requires your presence tonight, my Caius. The party is for your master, S. Julius Frontinus. It'll be all boring politics and campaigns for them – but we young blades may drink and wench in between waiting on our masters.'

Everyone in this little group appeared to know this young cockscomb. Marcus did not. He studied the fellow – patrician, contemptuous, hair oiled and curled, white tunic cut perfectly, gilded sandals, pomander and tablets at waist, his flesh rosy and recently bathed and scraped and oiled – a fine popinjay. But in the heavy set of the features, the way the lines from nostrils curved down to the edges of the mouth, the lift of the eyebrows as Gnaeus's gaze rested on Marcus, Britannicus knew this man was dangerous.

'Oh, yes, Gnaeus,' Pomponius said, swiftly, a trifle breathlessly. 'I must introduce you – this is M. Julius Britannicus – my Julius, I have the honour to present Gn. Flavius Paulinus, presently come from Britain—'

'Yes, yes,' broke in Flavius Paulinus. 'And I still talk of the old man as the governor of Britain. But that'll be your master now, eh, my Pomponius, eh?'

Marcus normally now, having grown in years, did not allow himself to like or dislike anyone on the instant of first meeting. But, as Mithras knew, he did it all the time.

He detested this blot, at once, instantly, and without recourse to reason.

'Britannicus, eh?' Gnaeus Flavius Paulinus stared disdainfully at Marcus.

'I have just come from Syria, from Judaea,' said Marcus in his young-old voice, gravely.

'Oh, aye, whoring with the Jewesses, I'll be bound.'

At this Flavius Martinus laughed, and repeated his jest about the drabs' knives, and the young men laughed, freely and easily, men of the world, their careers before them, lighthearted. They formed a glittering group, there with the sunshine falling from the high openings, standing in negligent postures on the marble floors, their slaves not too far off to respond instantly to the slightest whim of their masters.

'As you know, I've just come from Britain. My, how we chased the barbarians! Those Brigantes thought to build a fortress and defy us! But the old man soon showed them the error of their ways. The boys were up at the walls and over and their swords drank so much blood – you should have seen it!' He smacked his lips at the memory.

The conversation centred around this Flavius Paulinus, and of his dashing assistance to the governor of Britain, Q. Petillius Cerialis, who was a personal friend and relative of Vespasian. The name of Legio XX came up, and of its legate, Agricola; but nothing was said of Marcus's father, and he could relax. The talk sickened him. The army had marched and, without building too many marching camps, had smashed the Brigantes. Marcus knew them well enough. They were a tribe with whom there had been much trouble in the old days. His mother's people, the Iceni, knew about that.

But – what was this fool saying?

'. . . slit all their throats – men, women, children. The women were like fiends, tearing their hair, their clothes. By the Names, it was a fine sight. It must have rivalled the battle in which this Boadicea was exterminated.' Flavius Paulinus paused a moment for the obvious to sink in. Marcus, certainly, knew what the bastard was talking about.

When his great aunt – whose name was Boudicca – had risen with the tribes, and been defeated at the end, Petillius Cerialis, then legate of Legio IX Hispana, had been cut up with a vexillation of the legion and forced to retire. Catus Decianus, the procurator, fled to Gaul. The legate of Legio II Augusta being absent, the praefectus castrorum, one Poenius Postumus, had refused to march, fearing ambush. So the campaign had been left to C. Suetonius Paulinus. He it was who had smashed Boudicca.

Now this upstart Flavius Paulinus was commenting on that and comparing that old battle with what he had recently been doing against the Brigantes, destroying them in the same blood and guts way.

These patricians, these equestrians, bright life-loving young men, brilliant, were talking and laughing about it all. The tribes of Britain were separate and distinct, and many had no cause to love any of the others. The Silures were giving trouble, so Marcus gathered, and were ripe for conquest. And, then –

'. . . a snivelling parcel of Iceni, mixed with 'em. Aye! We showed them what being Roman means! They are at peace with us, the Iceni, are they not, after – you know! So the lads went in with the gladius. The men fought and the children had necks wrung, and the women—'

Here Paulinus paused for effect.

'Go on! Go on!' clamoured the others, agog.

Paulinus chuckled. 'Oh, we served 'em with weapons, all right. But not iron gladii! No! We served 'em all with a better weapon than that. And, after it was done and they'd run shrieking, their clothes ripped off, their hair blowing every which way, the blood running down their legs, why, then they were fine sport! Javelins! The old pilum stuck 'em like pigs, all snorting and squealing, the pila in their bellies. I tell you, by the Names! It was as fine a sight as any I've seen—'

Paulinus glanced at Marcus with a quick savage toss of the head.

'What ails you, my friend? Have you a weak stomach?'

Somehow, Marcus said: 'I was at Masada.'

He had to control himself. Had to. There were ways and ways. But Paulinus talked remorselessly on.

'A chieftainess with 'em. Beautiful piece. All silky hair, and a body – not young, mind you, but not old. She was class, a real princess. The lads knew their place. They saved her for us, for the officers. The primus pilus himself brought her into us. We'd been drinking – you know. It was a riot. She didn't plead. She just stood there – tall and straight – gods!' Here Paulinus broke off and wiped sweat from his forehead. He was excited at memories. Marcus held himself stiff, rigid. It couldn't be. It just could not be.

Paulinus laughed and said, not quite steadily: 'We ploughed her furrow – not that it hadn't been ploughed before, mark you. She'd had children. But she said not a word. Not a word, Jupiter take her!'

The others interjected inflamed questions, demanding to know more. This story appealed to them. This, they understood. This was what the Roman wars were all about; power and wealth and sex, the taking of all three when and wherever possible, from those who were too weak to hold and guard them.

'By Venus! She was a morsel!' Paulinus recovering from

that shattering memory-blast waxed enthusiastic. He saw that he had no need to exaggerate to impress the others. Trulls and drabs; they were the fodder of the Legions. But a real chieftainess, dragged into the tribune's tent, used by those light-hearted, brilliant rapscallions, the gilded youth of Rome. How this proved the might of Imperial Rome!

Marcus moved away.

He moved away.

Had he not done so he would have leaped on this brilliant patrician, this Gnaeus Flavius Paulinus and taken his throat in his fists and crushed the life out of the bastard.

'Six of 'em!' declared Paulinus, confident now, joking, making crude and obscene references that kept his audience in fits of laughter. 'If you don't count old Crassus — he wiggled away when we'd done, like a fish on a hook—' They all bellowed their merriment at the image.

Marcus became aware that his fingers were biting into his palms, his own finger nails that were kept trimmed clean and short, like a legionary's. He had to relax. His mother was a princess of the Iceni and she would know this poor woman who had been so vilely violated. He wondered who it might have been; Boudicca herself had seen her own two daughters ravished by Romans. And yet — and yet in the greater context, the glory of Rome, the breath of civilization, weren't they the real things that counted? Long gone were the days when Marcus had been a trembling boy, filled with ideals. The disgrace and death of his father had left scars and a burning hatred; he had matured every day not only in mind and body, but in spirit since then.

When a chariot carried a great general in his triumph, could he concern himself over the ant who was crushed beneath those bedecked wheels? For the pacification of his island home, Marcus knew there must be wars and battles, that men and women must die before the true peace that Rome could bring might enfold the land in quietness.

He became aware of Pomponius walking over to him, smiling.

'You've piqued Flavius Paulinus,' Pomponius said. 'He would like to hear about Masada at first hand, from one who was there.'

'Yes.'

'From one end of the empire to the other. Paulinus doubts

that Masada was as tough a task as is made out. He seems to think the victory over the Brigantes presented more obstacles.'

'Yes.'

'At least,' said Pomponius, baffled. 'He has said that the enemies the legions of Britain fought, fought. They did not slit their throats, like the enemies of the Tenth.'

'It was the Ninth, was it not, in Britain? I wonder what will happen to them, in the end.'

'Marcus! Are you ill?'

'No – no, Pomponius, my friend. I was thinking – but, no matter. Yes, I will come to this party tonight, and mayhap this puppy Flavius Paulinus will convince me the Ninth had a sterner task than the Tenth.'

'The Twentieth were there, also, Marcus.'

'Ah! The Twentieth!'

'Until tonight, then?'

'Until tonight.'

The orgy was in full swing and M. Julius Britannicus was sick of the sight and sound of it.

Not that he hadn't perked up at the rounded glowing forms of the girls they'd brought in. Clad in light flowing draperies, transparent so that all their glory of form shone through, the girls had danced and sung and made their provocative gestures, and now, amid the overturned wine goblets and the fallen chaplets, the brave young bloods were hard at it.

With the vomitorium handy so that they might empty their stomachs and thus cram down a whole fresh meal, they had eaten and eaten. The drink had only partially fuddled them. Many lamps shone down on the wanton scene. Rugs draped the marble floor and gilded couches stood ready to receive the owners of tottering legs. Flower petals scattered everywhere and the mingled scents suffused the air with perfume. Slaves chosen for their beauty or for their deformed ugliness scuttered about, bringing in more wine, taking away the asses after their performance – a group of flushed youths diced hard, wagering vast sums that would be recouped from the bleeding backs of their slaves and from the skilled fingers of their workers.

A sprite clad only in a slipping length of transparent pink silk accosted Marcus, pulling his tunic, trying to get at him. Her face, painted, shone with sweat. She was not fully drunk;

but had drunk enough to make her past wantonness to the point where she would have thrown herself at a camel, instead of an ass, had there been one handy.

'Come, my Hercules! Let me see your club!'

He pushed her away; but she clung, laughing shrilly.

Pomponius wandered over, staggering crookedly, slopping wine. He giggled. 'Hercules! By Venus – the wench is right, Marcus. You are the hardest man I've met in many a year.'

'Can't you take her away, my Pomponius? Can't you plough a fresh furrow?'

Pomponius laughed again, and drank, and hurled the goblet wildly from him. It struck a passing slave behind the ear, and the girl fell, blood gushing from her nostrils. She was dragged out hurriedly by her fellow slaves. Hardly anybody noticed and nobody cared.

'Another is beyond even me, now, my Julius. I've—'

'There are oysters there – something that Britain can provide more nobly than—'

'Oysters! Ah, Lucius Licinius Lucullus has much to answer for! The old rogue! Anyway, I've lost all faith in 'em. I've eaten two dozen this very night, and—'

'And?' said Marcus, giving the girl a robust push on her admittedly delightful bottom, so that she squealed and slid on a rug across the polished marble floor. The walls around glowed in the lamplight, painted with scenes of carnival and fiesta and debauch, most of them no more abandoned than the reality on the floor, if more artistic.

'And, indeed!'

'So?'

'Five!' said Pomponius, looking vastly proud.

'Wait an hour, is my advice, my Pomponius. A small hour. Then try again. The cedars of Lebanon do not grow in a night.'

The debauch racketted on; but nothing new was on show tonight. The elders, the men of empire and business, had gone long since, and, if the truth were known, they were probably helling it up in their own way, with their own set and their own women, in secluded apartments of one or other of their villas. Rome was filled with luxury and decadence and pleasure alone mattered to these men. Women, as well. The mysteries gave ample scope for the young pale men so beloved by the matrons, in their secrets and their furtive gigglings and whisperings – or

36

so Marcus was given to understand, having a care for his private parts.

Over on a saffron rug three girls were expertly manipulating the supine form of Gnaeus Flavius Paulinus. Every now and then he gave a grunt and then a drunken giggle.

Pomponius, looking, said: 'He is a dangerous man, my Julius.'

'How does that touch me?'

'It was noted. How your face went black with fury when he boasted of what he had done in the country of the Brigantes.'

'Brigantia is not my country.' Marcus's voice was flat and leaden. 'How could it be? Am I not a Roman?'

'No one has denied that – Marcus. No one. And your work with Flavius Silva has been recognized.'

'Oh, that, yes. The phalera has been bestowed, I grant—'

He could wear the medal, fixed to his breastplate as a Roman officer. Some of the older centurions had phalerae plastered all across their chests.

A girl, quite naked and with streaming hair, ran shrieking past them. Her shrieks changed to shouts of laughter as the two pursuing men caught her. They swung her about, tossing her into the air, catching her, and then tumbling her on the floor, like a liburna, fore and aft, with all her oars stirring the sea into flying foam.

'A liburna has only two banks of oars!' yelled a flushed youth, sitting up and crushing a bunch of grapes so that the juice ran over his hair and face and neck. 'In the old days the Greeks used triremes! Three banks of oars!'

'Well,' shouted the girl, gasping, and laughing and giggling. 'What! Do you tarry with your grapes, or are you like Silenus, all grape and no do?'

Pomponius roared out his enjoyment and a little crowd gathered about the thrashing forms on the carpets. Marcus, amused, of course, stirred himself to move away. If nothing particularly interesting happened soon he'd take himself off.

The wine he'd drunk had done nothing for him. He had insisted that it be properly watered, as was civilized; but some of the young fools, notably this very same G. Flavius Paulinus, had taken up the barbarian habit of drinking unwatered wine. They deserved all that Dionysus would bring upon them. From a great height.

As though mirroring his thoughts, he heard a choking grunt to his side and, turning, saw Paulinus freed from the girls heaving up his guts in great foul swashes of liquid across the floor. With a grimace of distaste, Marcus moved away.

'By Bacchus!' called Paulinus. He snatched the linen from a slave and wiped his mouth. 'That's better. I'll have the architect flogged who built the vomitorium so far away!'

This was enough. Marcus enjoyed a good orgy like any decent fellow. But he was growing more and more particular about the company he cared to keep. Pomponius was a good enough fellow, a little light in the reasoning cohort, and a little forward in the friendship cohort; but his cohort that dealt with future interest was powerful enough to make Marcus suffer the young blood. And, to be honest, old Pomponius wasn't all that bad.

But – this Flavius Paulinus . . .

'Stay, Britannicus! I want to hear about Masada!'

'There is little to tell.' Marcus spoke formally, stiffly, wanting to put a boot into the other's guts. And not doing so for obvious reasons.

'Well, there is much to tell of Brigantia! By Venus! How we slaughtered them!'

He came over and Marcus was forced out of decency, for despite his iron-hardness in battle he was still a young man, to sit down and listen. The Parisi, friends of Rome, had been something instrumental in the overthrow of the Brigantes. These Brigantes, a rough and crude lot, although with many valuable items to their credit, as Marcus knew, ruled the land from sea to sea, and although once a client kingdom, it was clear that Rome saw more profit in subjecting them and colonizing. Northwards of them lived the Votadini, the Selgovae, the Damnonii and the Novantae – Roman names, not the names his Celtic mother, Princess Elfleda of the Iceni, had told him when describing the tribes of the island.

'You're a black indrawn fellow, Julius Britannicus! I had thought, with your name, you would welcome news from the pestilential land of mist.'

'Yes. It is very different from Syria, although the work we did at Masada sounds similar to yours beating Venutius. His great camp could not stand against the legions, as Masada could not.'

'Aye! And after – did I tell you of the Iceni? Their luscious

38

chieftainess? A real beauty – fire and hauteur, not a cry, not a plea for mercy—'

'You slew her, then, after . . .?'

'Oh – I do not know, and care not, by Venus! She was tumbled into the dung heap, I don't doubt, her throat slit.'

'After you – six of you, you said?'

'That's right. She was lush, lush, a real Juno!'

'Nobody else apart from you six and – Crassus, was it?'

'That's right.'

And Paulinus described the scene again, going into details, telling it over.

Somehow, Marcus received the distinct impression that the young braggart lived with that scene. It obsessed him. The beautiful woman, a virtuous matron, a princess, tall and statuesque, like a Juno – and her clothes stripped from her, and the lascivious hands of the drunken young tribunes throwing her upon the table, and holding her down as, one by one –

'Although, as Venus is my witness, she did not struggle or cry out. She lay there as though she did not care, but I'll warrant she did! It was as though she was gone from us then – witched, I guess, by her everlastingly damned Druids.'

Yes, Marcus saw, Paulinus would never rid his heart of that sight.

'Her name?' Paulinus coughed and bellowed irritably and a slave girl ran across with a filled wine goblet. He drank and wiped the back of his hand across his mouth. 'Her name, Julius? How by Bacchus do I know? Wait – one of these damned tongue-twisting names – Fedolia, something like that – who cares?'

Marcus sat forward.

Paulinus swilled the wine, staring at the ruby surface, brooding. 'Damned witch! Her eyes! Brown and shining – I can see them still!' He banged his fist on to his knee so that the wine jumped and stained the front of his white tunic. 'Stay! I remember. One of the legionaries said something – I think he'd been transferred from the Twentieth – yes, something – oh, I forget what. But he told me her name – yes, I have it.'

'Yes?' said Marcus Julius Britannicus.

'The Princess Elfleda, of the Iceni.'

THREE

Strolling along to the Baths the next day, ready to make the most of the remaining few days in Rome before Frontinus set off for Britain, Marcus watched everything going on, from the hurrying slaves to the great ladies borne past in their slave-carried litters. More than one pair of dark eyes regarded him from the close curtains, and more than one girlish heart palpitated at sight of his broad shoulders and defiant, erect carriage, the limber strength of him.

Oblivious of these girlish swellings of emotion, Marcus pushed on, munching the bunch of grapes he had just bought, listening to all the turmoil and bustle of the greatest city on Earth.

Just before he turned into the Baths he was met by Pomponius. The young man wore a fine tunic, as did Marcus, and he was all ready for the Baths. But, instead of turning in straight away, he fairly ran up to Marcus, his open face filled with stark wonder at his news.

'You've heard, Marcus? The news?'

'Domitian slept well, and ate a hearty breakfast—'

'No. No, you clown! This is serious.'

'I have but just risen from a virtuous night's sleep. Tell me, my Pomponius, tell me your earth-shattering news.'

'It is no joke, Marcus! By Bacchus! My head! That party, may Hades claim 'em all!' Then, abruptly sobered by his own words, he stammered out: 'Well, I did not mean that, exactly. Well, not that at all.'

'Stop mumbling and maundering, my dear Pomponius. If you have news that prevents me from going into the Baths, then, for the sake of the Names, tell me!'

'No – I mean, yes. Let us go in. I do not think I shall risk the hottest of the hot baths today, my Julius. Something a little more delicate for the sake of my health.'

'I intend to leap into the coldest bath they can provide, and swim as hard as I can, for an hour, and then I shall feel my insides purged.'

'You are a barbarian.'

'Well, my Pomponius.' They were entering the lofty entrance hall, and already the particular sensuous inner life of the Baths was beginning to flow over them, despite the raucous shouts of vendors and hawkers and pimps and tricksters. 'Tell me this so great news, or must my ears hang out until they fall off?'

'Flavius Martinus told me early – he is being asked many questions, for they went along together, after the party.'

'They did? How interesting. *Who* did, my dear idiot?'

'Why, Flavius Martinus and Flavius Paulinus.'

'Well, go on—'

'It's Gnaeus! It's horrible, my dear Julius, perfectly horrible! They told me everything – and I was sick—'

'What did they tell you?'

If the words were perhaps sharper than before, Pomponius did not notice in the memory of his anguish.

'They found him – in an alley – he was barely recognizable. He'd had his genitals torn out – torn out, they said, not cut off – torn out and stuffed into his – his mouth, and—'

The racket of the Baths was all around them, now, the enormously lofty ceilings catching the sounds, hollowly, and tossing them back, soft and sharp, intense, filling that vast enclosed space with a continuous chirruping succession of sound. The two young men walked along, and Pomponius looked at the marble slabs, at his sandals, and did not look at his companion.

'Go on,' said Marcus.

'He had been – he had been – broken. By Venus, Marcus! I did not know what they meant, when they told me. He was shapeless, they said, with his eyes dangling on stalks, gouged out, and all his teeth smashed, and his nose crushed – and his mouth, well, his mouth—'

'Yes, they wouldn't have seen his mouth, at first.'

'He had been beaten black and blue – and he couldn't cry out—'

'I should have thought a man being beaten would cry out.'

'You don't understand. His tongue had been torn out by the roots.'

'Oh, of course. To make way for the—'

'Marcus!' Pomponius looked up, his swimming eyes regarding Marcus with a puzzled stare that warned that the situation was toppling into something fresh and dangerous. 'You seem – distant, my Julius – as though you—'

'I am horrified, my Pomponius. It is dreadful. One thinks that since the Flavians one is safe to walk the streets – not like in Nero's time, or the Republic – or—'

'He's dead, dead, mutilated, torn. It's the work of a savage, a barbarian, a madman!'

'Oh, yes,' said Marcus Julius Britannicus. 'It is the work of a madman, without a doubt. And a savage barbarian, too, I expect. Yes, I quite see that.'

'And they don't know who – or what – it could have been. It couldn't have been an escaped wild animal. Ah – there is Maxilius – I must have a word with him. His family have a villa near poor Paulinus's. He may know something.'

Pomponius hurried off.

Marcus stared after him, and then turned into the inner rooms of the Baths. The plunge into the icy cold waters would come vastly refreshing on this particular morning.

Of course, he had known at once.

The moment Paulinus had begun to speak, there in the inner room of the Palaestra, he had known.

And, of course, he had not believed. How could he believe? How could any son believe a thing so monstrous?

Those moments when he'd waited, cloak drawn to his eyes, waiting for Flavius Martinus to shout drunken farewells to Flavius Paulinus, with the link-slaves waiting, too – and the quick dash, and the grasp and seizure, and the link-slaves running and screaming, their torches going sizzlingly smash on the stones. Yes, he remembered that.

Quite what had happened thereafter was hazy. He remembered warm wet stickiness. He recalled that his dagger lay snugged to his waist throughout. There was little he did remember until his fouled clothes had been burned in the dead darkness of the night and he had gone to sleep, burned internally himself, purged.

But – purged of only one of six, plus Crassus.

Five others – and at the orgy Paulinus, boastfully, had given him their names.

Well, five men there were who would go the same way as Gnaeus Flavius Paulinus.

And, of the five, four at least were still in Britain.

He was due to ship out with Frontinus, the new pro praetor

42

of Britain, and nothing he wished for would change that. He must go on the special duty he was charged with, of the same nature as that he had performed working for Flavius Silva, out there in Judaea. This time, instead of scouting in a hot land scoured by burning winds under a brazen sky, he would be scouting in the rainy meadows and green forests of his own land, the land of mist.

Nothing he could do would change that. He could get to these four men no faster way than travelling with a new governor going out to his province. There would be a retinue. In that glittering assemblage of men Marcus would be insignificant, a mere aide, to be used in moments of difficulty with the natives.

That, with great satisfaction, was just how M. Julius Britannicus would have it.

A wild beast hunted best from concealment.

Sextus Julius Frontinus was most anxious to reach Britain as quickly as posssible. Since the return of Cerialis the legates would have been holding the forts.

When the brilliant cavalcade rode through Gaul Marcus heard Frontinus expatiating on his part in the Gallic rebellion, and of how whilst being a fair man he would stand no nonsense from the painted savages of Britain. At least, considered Marcus, Petillius Cerialis had served earlier in Britain, and did have some understanding. But he hoped for much from this new man, this S. Julius Frontinus. The man was a Julian, and that had helped Marcus in this appointment, when the Flavians ran everything. Frontinus had been praetor five years earlier, and was well on the road of a distinguished career. Britain could be the making or breaking of him for the very highest commands.

From Gesoriacum they made a reasonably swift passage to Dubris, a passage on which Pomponius was vastly sick, to Marcus's amusement. He was not shocked that he could still laugh, could still walk and talk and act like a normal human being. The madness was contained. The savage barbarity that Pomponius had so rightly said marked the man who slew Paulinus was tightly rammed down into a heart set like iron. Coldness and fire, violent anger and cunning calculation worked together in Marcus to produce a self-contained equanimity that reassured him that all would be paid for in the end. There was

43

time. There was no need to hurry. Particularly, there was no need to hurry the final rites.

No need at all.

There had been the usual questions from the aediles of the city prefect, and no doubt the men of the urban cohort would still be talking of the horrid murder. Perhaps, even, the great mass of plebs might give it a word or two; but as Marcus knew only too well, the Games would dominate everyone's thoughts and actions, leaving little room for much else.

So, following along in the resplendent cavalcade after the new governor, Marcus rode into Londinium. After his great-aunt's destruction the place had been put back together again with furious energy. The old capital – still that, in theory – of Camulodunum, also, was being restored. Verulamium lay still in a messy state of ashes and fallen rubble, so Marcus had been told. Well, these were marks of his family's vengeance. He wished he might have been riding into Londinium with its walls razed and the ashes blowing; that starkness would have fitted the mood he kept battened down beneath his bland, cheerful, efficient young equerry's appearance.

Glevum no longer served as the main legionary fortress in the southwest. Now Isca further to the west served that function, and pointed the way into the heart of the Silures where, amid steep mountains and valleys, much fighting lay ahead.

Very considerately, in view of the governor's evident desire to hurry to this coming confrontation with the Silures and to finish what had been begun and then abandoned some fifteen years ago, the cavalcade took their journey by way of Aquae Sulis. The place was very small, a mere spa, but Pomponius, egged on by Nepos, a harum-scarum scion of a proud equestrian family, and one of Frontinus's cohors amicorum, declared roundly that he would find the whitest whore in the best brothel and ride until morning.

'You'll find plenty of oysters in Britain,' said Marcus.

Nepos, somewhat fat for a young man who must be constantly on the move against his master's orders, chuckled. 'By Venus, Marcus, you're the right man to have here in this damned country.'

'I am here as a scout, as well you know.'

'Aye, Marcus. The other stratores don't know what to make of you.'

Well, that suited Marcus. The stratores, the equerries, had various functions in the retinue of the governor, and it suited both him and Frontinus if his own role was obscure. Flavius Silva had evidently written in detail to Frontinus when the new governor of Britain had agreed to take the young Britannicus on to his staff. Highly-placed men needed sharp but hidden tools. How that suited Marcus, in particular, of course, could never be revealed.

The cross would be light as a punishment.

So the laughing procession drew rein where old King Bladud had made his great discovery back in the mists of the past. Hustling grooms and hostlers assisted the Romans and amid a great bustling and flaring of torches — for they had ridden late through this land that had been pacified by the iron of the legions — went into the quarters assigned to them.

Once the tiresome formalities were dispensed with, Pomponius and Nepos sought Marcus and, laughing, drew him into the star-speckled night to sample the life of Aquae Sulis and discover what a small provincial spa might offer in the way of dissipation.

Nothing loath, for his thoughts tortured him despite that iron resolve to let vengeance run slow and deep and sure, Marcus went with them.

The girl with Marcus moaned softly and gripping him fiercely dragged him down. Marcus went willingly. He did not know if the girl was feigning or not; it didn't matter.

A terra-cotta lamp obscenely decorated with prancing goats and nymphs cast a flickering light into the small white-washed chamber. There was no window. Drapes at the door hung still. Outside the bark of a dog sounded high and shrill, as though he had been disturbed dreaming of rabbits.

'Come to me, come to me, strong, strong,' murmured the girl, clutching Marcus.

'Easy, easy,' he said. In this as in his vengeance he had no wish to be rushed. The longer it took, the more protracted the time, the sweeter the fruit.

He supposed Pomponius Endor was managing very well, considering the number of oysters he had swallowed down.

Nepos, too, in his rapscallion way would be plunging about, making a great deal of fuss and noise and being spent in no time at all. Well, Marcus had learned a great deal in his nineteen years.

When he had satisfactorily finished the girl lay back legs sidelong over the palliasse, her arms flung wide. She looked at him sleepily from smudged eyes. She might be a drab; but she was a real human being, too, so that Marcus placed extra sestertii on the low table with its cheap bowls, its brass mirror, its pottery jars of ointments and paints, its tweezers, its strigils, all the clutter of a woman's boudoir. There was going to be little refinement, out here on the frontier.

Although, to be sure, this place like most of southern Britain was rapidly acquiring the Roman gloss, and living in a security very real. Wild and savage barbarian tribes were living not many miles away from here, tribes that had on more than one occasion smashed and routed a legion. The presence of the legions, however, between the civilized and the non-civilized made all the difference.

Aquae Sulis, named for the goddess Minerva whom the Britons had for centuries worshipped as Sulis – her image frowned menacingly down from the pediment over by the baths – lay in this cup of woodlands, flowing down from the hills. No place for a legion, really; Marcus felt that he would welcome most wonderfully the sight of the legion, the standards, the eagle. The eagle! No matter what legion, the eagle meant something to any man who had served with the legions.

He rose and stretched and expanded his rib cage and became aware of the girl sitting up on the bed with its lumpy palliasse, staring up at him. Her face expressed something Marcus could not quite finger. Her breasts hung, round and fat and white, and yet, he saw, her nipples were erect and brightly, naturally red under their paint. She breathed quickly.

'You are a man, Roman.'

'As to that, girl, you are a woman.'

This pleased her.

She picked up a sestertius and bit it, and held it in her palm, idly tossing it up and down. Marcus pulled on his light woollen breeks and tied them, picked up his tunic. His cloak lay over a nail by the curtain.

As he buckled on his gladius, the sword in a neat but not gaudy scabbard of wood and leather and brass fittings, with a real silver chape and locket, the girl drew in her breath.

Marcus had brilliant and scarlet memories of a whore and a

gladius, far away, where the sun scoured the eyelids off a man, instead of gluing them down to his cheeks with mist.

He went out, saying over his shoulder as he reached down his cloak and draped it over his left arm: 'Mayhap, if we do not march tomorrow, I shall come again.'

The girl tossed the sestertius.

'You will be welcome, master.'

He had been gentle with her; he did not think he had been over-gentle. The way she had looked at his body, though – strange, unsettling . . .

Outside in the narrow little paved street with the shuttered shops and brothels and tiny factories it was raining. He put his head down into it and tried to avoid the puddles between the slabs. They were mostly new stone, though, from the local hills, and had not been worn into hollows where the water collected.

Most of the best places had been taken by the governor and his high officials. Bright blades like Marcus and the others of the cohors amicorum, men selected particularly by the governor to serve him in a variety of ways – old Septimus would have already chosen the best girl to drag up there, Marcus supposed, without rancour – these young men could either have their tents pitched or find holes in the public inn, or do whatever they damned liked so long as they did nothing to embarrass the governor.

He heard the scrape of shoe leather, harsh, at his back, and took no notice for three long strides.

Then the quality of the sound, bright above the splash of the rain, drew his attention.

That was no foppish civilian sandal, that was no simple leather-soled shoe; that was an iron-studded boot, a legionary boot, a caliga, from which the legionaries derived their nickname.

He whirled.

The three nearly had him.

They rushed now that he had turned and could see them, dim shadowed forms in the starlight, the moon humping golden and ghostly through the rain, the clouds passing high. They rushed and star glitter bounced from their extended blades.

At once Marcus saw he was in for a fight.

They bore down on him with swords in their fists, the gladius, the short and deadly stabbing sword of the legion.

His own blade whispered from the scabbard.

Well – he remembered what old Argos, the gladiator who

47

had taught him so much, used to say. He had learned enough since then to know he could out-play Argos without trouble. But the advice was still sound. Silently, Marcus leaped to meet the would-be assassins, his brand a sliver of cold steel in the starlight.

He whirled the cloak over his left arm, the cloak that providentially he had only begun to hang from its ornate clasps. He smothered the left-hand fellow's sword, sent him staggering on the slippery stones to collide with his fellow. That left the one on the right hand, who came in with every intention of finishing the fight quickly.

Marcus swirled the blade in best arena style, brought the cloak back, jumped to his right and so, leaning forward, passed the sword through the fellow's guts.

He did not stop to see the dark blood gush.

Instantly he had swung about and the blades of the other two rang against his own.

For a moment they hacked at him and he skipped and jumped about, fending them off, getting the cloak ready.

He sensed they were freedmen, perhaps by this deed even earning their freedom. They were active enough; but they lacked the finesse even a legionary learned who wished not to have his hide striped by his centurion, or his throat slit by the first barbarian he encountered in the line.

'Die, you bastard!' one of them grunted, and slashed wildly.

The uncharacteristic blow took Marcus all but by surprise.

The keen edge of the gladius barely missed his shoulder.

But the blow had opened up the whole side of the attacker.

Without thought, Marcus's gladius went in, just beneath the ribs. He twisted the blade and withdrew and swirled the cloak at the last one.

This one, white blank face shining with rain and sweat, came in, gasping, his gladius probing, his black hair falling over his forehead, like tendrils of vines. Marcus could guess what orders they had received. They were to kill this upstart Britannicus. They were not to return to report failure. If they did so they would be butchered out of hand.

So, for this man, it was kill or be killed.

He would not run away.

Kill or be killed!

That was the kind of harsh credo that had been bolted to Marcus his whole life. There was nothing new in that.

Marcus had no intention of killing this man.

He swung his sword at the fellow's head and then jumped back as the man made no attempt to guard himself but leaped in, snarling with his own fear, attempting to run Marcus through.

So a problem presented itself.

The wine Marcus had drunk earlier, the woman, the feel of the rain, the slither and clang of the blades, all blended in Marcus to make of him a man above himself. He settled down. This was something he did superlatively well. He did not want to kill this one – oh no! This one he wanted to take by the throat and choke a little and ask the very necessary questions that must be asked.

With an acrobatic leap that would have pleased any retiarius of the arena, he leaped and swung the cloak and so brought the fellow to his knees, gobbling with fear. But with that fear so strong upon him the man had changed hands, he now held the gladius in his left fist, and he was trying to stab upwards at Marcus's groin. With a practised step, Marcus avoided that, and swung his own sword in, flat.

Flat. Like a bludgeon.

The man gulped and stumbled back, tearing the cloak with him. He half-fell again, and again righted himself. Without an instant's hesitation he freed himself of the cloak, put his gladius into line and hurled himself forward.

A little frown appeared between Marcus's eyebrows.

The exercise was enjoyable, undeniably. But he should have finished it by now . . .

Many a legionary, many a secutor in the arena, was finished if he lost his shield. Old Argus, serving his father with devoted loyalty, had insisted he learn to fight with a gladius alone. The lessons were hard-learned and had proved invaluable.

Now Marcus wove a dazzling net, his blade flicking in to bring tiny spots of blood upon the face and arms of his opponent. The man was breathing in stertorous gasps that rasped through his wide-open mouth. His grey tunic hung belted upon him. His heavy boots scraped the flags. Now the tip of Marcus's sword brought forth heavier gouts of blood as he was forced to battle fiercely to drive the other off. He was determined not to kill him. Yet the would-be assassin made that difficult. He was intent on slaying this bright young patrician or on being slain himself.

The difficulty of that grew moment by moment. It was, in truth, a pretty problem. Argos would have been overjoyed at the contest, and have been urging encouragement and advice.

But then, they'd have been using the rudis, the wooden sword...

This must be the moment...

The man slashed wildly and then, with a despairing display of skill, brought his gladius into line and thrust. Marcus sidestepped, then, with the swift lunge of the eagle, stepped in. He brought his knee up into the man's crotch, grabbed the right wrist in his own left hand, and smashed the flat of the blade to the fellow's temple.

The man went down like felled oak.

He was not unconscious; there would not be time for that. He scrabbled around, and Marcus took his chin in his left hand and forced the filthy bearded face up.

'Who sent you, dog?'

Only a mumble, a mumble and a trickle of blood over the chin and over Marcus's gripping fingers.

'Tell me, tell me now!'

'Mithras take you!'

'I think Mithras is with me, dog, and not you.'

The fellow slumped. Marcus bent again, twisting, and saw the hollowed cheeks, the exhaustion, the closed eyes. He cursed. He let go and stood up. Well, there must be an inquiry. The magistrates must be informed. What lay behind this had to be cleared up.

The man moved.

He moved like a crippled crab, disjointed, heaving. He hunched up, his grey tunic curved, spattered with rain, stained.

Marcus saw, and leaped. Too late. The man had the pommel of the sword wedged into a crack between the flags. He fell. He fell and thrust himself down and the point of the gladius burst into his belly, into his guts, broke through in a gouting weltering of blood and intestines.

Marcus cursed. He turned the body over with his feet.

'By Mithras! The dog has escaped me!'

Yet, for all that, it had been nobly done.

The man was almost dead. Blood gushed from his mouth, all black and shining. His face showed a smoothing of those hollows of defeat, the bristly cheeks filling in death.

Turning away, Marcus picked up his cloak. The magistrates, yes, they must be told . . .

The javelin took him in the left forearm, through the cloak. He felt the shock and the burning pain. He looked down stupidly. Already the pilum was bent behind the head, bending so that it could not be hurled back. Marcus staggered, and the second javelin whirred past.

He could not see in the rain, the bars of water struck the paving and bounced in little bubbles. He bent his head, and swerved drunkenly, and ran. He ran. He ran from the open straight street, away from those deadly javelins, ran into the shadows.

Only when he was well away did he pause for breath.

And then his first words were: 'By Mithras! I'll have the bastards!'

The horses jogged to the crest and halted, blowing, and there, below them, lay the sea.

Marcus stared at the grey tumbled waters without expression. Romans did not like the sea. But he would feel some affinity for that never-still expanse, always changing, hiding its secrets so well, bright or sullen, calm or ferociously angry. The cavalcade dipped down over the grass. These men with the new governor of Britain made a bright cavalcade, with glittering armour, brave feathers, high-spirited horses, and with the baggage train following on and carrying all the luxuries they considered essential.

A man broke from the cover off to their right, running with a staggering panting exhaustion. His arms and legs, spider-thin, jerked with the intense effort of staying on his feet and running. He wore merely a filthy breechclout. His left arm hung, dangling and useless, caked with dried blood.

No one needed to be told who or what he was.

Frontinus held up a hand and the cavalcade halted, the horses tossing their heads and blowing, the men breaking into excited observations of the sport.

The four horsemen pursuing the runaway prisoner would come up with him directly in front of the halted cavalcade.

They whooped as they whipped their mounts on. The horses were the small wiry hill-ponies of Britain, similar to those used for hauling the chariots; the four men bulked large on the horses' backs, making their menace more real, more frightening to the fugitive.

The business was conducted with the swift and callous efficiency to be expected.

If a prisoner or a slave ran, he would be pursued, taken up and punished.

The man went down, screaming, trying to shield his head from the whips with his right arm, his useless left arm dangling. Blood drops flew. The sounds of the blows reached across the grass, flat meaty thunkings, harsh and completely merciless. The bright young men in Frontinus's retinue began to complain that the slave had given no sport, had not run hard enough, had made nowhere nearly enough effort to waste their time like this.

'By the Names!' shouted Nepos, vastly excited, his fat face shaking. 'I would have wagered a bag of sestertes the fellow would have reached the water!'

'Then thank your Venus you did not, my Nepos!' called Pomponius, laughing.

The incident had enlivened the party. Their hunting blood was up. Someone yelled and a dozen voices took up the cry.

'Another one! No – two of them! After them!'

There was no holding the young men. Roaring and rollicking they dug in their heels and went galloping after the two fresh fugitives. These two had cleverly broken away from the path of the man who had been caught and were making for the beach. Down there would be coracles for them to steal. Now, thinking themselves past the three horsemen who were busily taking up their comrade, they were astonished and terrified to see a whole pack of new enemies riding hard down upon them, yelling and halloing.

Marcus, caught up with the excited mob, his horse bounding along without need of urging, found himself carried along pell-mell in the midst of the whirling mob of horsemen. He dragged back on the reins; but his horse, maddened by the shouts and the smells and the pack of horses hammering along all about him, dragged his head forward, twisting, refusing the reins.

Abruptly, Marcus let the ribbons go slack and dug his legs in firmly. He wouldn't torture the poor beast. He'd have to be unpleasant to his mount to make it stop now. Away they went, bounding over the springy turf, the whole pack shouting at the tops of their voices, whips flailing.

The two fugitives saw the horror about to burst upon them.

They ran.

Over the lip of grassland they scuttled like two coneys seeking their boltholes. They vanished from view but a dozen racing strides brought them into sight again, crabbing down the gravelly edge of the little scarp towards the beach. Stones clattered under the horses's hooves.

'The devil take it!' exclaimed Marcus, jolted furiously in his saddle, gripping on tenaciously. 'Someone—'

That someone was Nepos. The plump young man's horse skidded on a stone. The horse plunged one way, Nepos the other.

The rest thundered past. Now Marcus was sawing on the reins in real earnest; the horse with that subtle cunning of horses in times of crisis had got the bit between his teeth. His strong yellow teeth clamped on the bronze. Away he went and nothing was going to stop him short of a ballista bolt or a snare net.

'Idiots!' fumed Marcus. But there was no denying the sheer thrill of riding so close to destruction. The wind flattened into his face, the horse beneath him was all alive and vibrant, the plunging of his body jolting him so that he knew he was alive, could feel the hard hammer blows from his spine cracking up into his skull. He hung on, feeling anger growing in him against his own foolishness.

This beast was not Pluto, that magnificent black stallion given him by his father – Pluto had thrown a shoe and was back with the baggage train and Marcus would have the hide off the blacksmith if the job was not done aright – and this borrowed horse had a mean sideways jinking to his run that meant he'd try to have his rider off given the slightest weakness, the barest opportunity.

The reins felt slippery with sweat.

'Come hup, you brute!' Marcus hauled back, digging his heels in, gripping with his knees. The horse scrabbled away to his left, slipping and sliding on the loose stones. The runaways ahead were screaming now over the smashing noise of the pursuit; but Marcus's confounded horse was taking him away from them, angling like a monstrous crab along the pebbled beach.

If he was thrown off that would give Pomponius a good belly laugh.

Marcus was still young enough to resent being laughed at.

The wound he had taken from that would-be assassin's

pilum sprang into vivid hurtful life. Fresh blood welled through the bandages. Marcus cursed. He used his other arm to haul back and the horse's head curved around so that Marcus caught a foam-covered glimpse of his teeth, all strong and yellow, clamped firmly over the bronze.

The other riders had gone careering over the beach. A sprawled jumble of rocks and boulders impeded them and they poured around it, splashing into pools, cheering and hallooing, going like crazy men. The runaways staggered and gasped and then the whole scene vanished from Marcus's sight as his horse carried him fleetingly along the beach, headlong in a mad career that looked certain to end in destruction for the rider.

The wind of his passage battered at him. He hung on and then the anger erupted. By Mithras! He was no man to be thus tamely galloped away with! He clamped his teeth shut and ignored the pain in his arm. The reins slicked under his fingers and he hauled back, savagely, barbarously, not caring if the poor beast under him suffered for the space it would take to haul up.

In a wild screeching the horse twisted, his head reared up, sideways, the eyes flashing madly. Over went Marcus, skidding sideways, the horses' hooves lashing out, over and over he was flung, still gripping the reins, to come down with a rib-crunching thunk on to the pebbles.

He lay for a moment, winded, his eyes blurred, feeling the frenzied tugs on the reins as the horse tried to break free. He jerked the reins viciously. The horse snorted. Groaning as pains shot through his body, Marcus staggered to his feet. He gripped the reins and he stared at the horse, and he was minded to kick the damfool beast.

The horse whinnied at him and stood there, spraddle-legged, his head hanging down, all the puff gone from him.

Marcus felt his rage evaporate. He laughed. He had come out of it well enough, no bones broken and a few grazes and bruises to show, nothing for a man who marched with the legions.

The horse looked properly repentant now, blowing and moving his head from side to side. Marcus turned and there were two people, a man and a woman, hiding under the over-hanging lip of turf above the pebbles.

Instantly Marcus's sword came free of the scabbard, at once, without thought.

His first instinctive thought was that here were more hidden assassins seeking to slay him.

'Who are you?' He growled the words out, hard, making them forceful, and he emphasized them by an ominous pass with the sword.

The woman cowered back. The front of her frayed black robe was opened and she was giving suck to a babe. The man remained where he was; but he spread his hands imploringly. His hair was grey and scant; but his beard, although grey, hung luxuriantly and his robe, once white, showed traces of ornamentation.

'I beg you, my son, do not betray us.'

Marcus stared. The man spoke a barbarously accented Greek. Greek was the natural second tongue to any educated man. Marcus with his gladius ready stepped closer.

'Who are you?' he repeated, this time in Greek.

'My name is Pwyllelni. I am an adept. I see you are a Roman and yet I see more in you than that – for the sake of humanity I beg you. Do not betray us to those barbarians.'

'Romans are not barbarians!' said Marcus. He spoke sharply and he saw the woman flinch.

Then this Pwyllelni spoke again, and this time he spoke in a language that although Marcus did not fully understand bore so many allusions and common although twisted word-stocks to his mother's native tongue, that he could follow most of what was said.

'No, old man. I am a Roman—'

The man's lined face showed an exhaustion that would soon overwhelm the calm strength of him. Crouched in a hole in a bank, hiding – no, those were not his usual occupations.

Moved, Marcus said: 'My mother was of the Iceni.' And, having said that, he could not go on.

'We are of the Silures. The iron of Rome will destroy us; this I see. This my people know. But it is not meet in the destiny of any man that he should sink into nothingness without doing all a man may do to prevent the inevitable.'

Marcus nodded. There had been few Druids left in the part of Britain where the Romans had conquered. And, anyway, the Belgae had brought different customs, although all were Celts, and the Druids had moved with the migrations, westwards. When Suetonius had devastated the Druid sanctuaries far north of here only a fool would believe the religion had been obliterated.

'For all that, old man, I am a Roman and must give you up to your Roman masters.'

'And have you never sacrificed to Taranis? To Esus? Have you never hungered for the divination to give you what you most desire? Or do you believe in this nonsense of Zeus and his parasites?' Before Marcus could reply, Pwyllelni went on, speaking now with a savagery marked by the curl of his nostril and the lift of his head. 'Or perhaps you follow this weak-kneed curdling Nazarene? He will lead you from slavery into slavery—'

'I follow Mithras, like any legionary, and now you will stand up and I shall prod you along back to your captivity.'

The Druid did not stand up. He saw more in this young man than the young man could know himself of what potentialities lay within him. Pwyllelni lifted a finger and made a Sign.

'We are not Roman slaves. I am an adept and Rona is a priestess of the inner circle. We have been cruelly taken by these brutes – herded along, whipped, starved – and yet no man or woman of them can call us slave. I ask you again, you who are not a man branded with the foul iron of Rome – I beg you, do not betray us.'

Marcus felt the sword in his grip. Not branded with the iron of Rome! In that, this Druid was wrong . . .

But, all the same. If they were not slaves then no one could lose by them. And the woman was exhausted, her eyes deeply-sunk over great black smudges. She looked too thin and fragile to be giving suck to a babe, as though all her strength was being drained out of her.

'Hey, my Julius! Where has your beast taken you then, to Hades to sleep with the maidens of the pit?'

That was Pomponius. No doubt he had hoicked Nepos up and now he was after a guffaw at the expense of Marcus. The youthful arrogance of that Roman voice hardened Marcus. He looked at the old Druid, and his firmness of bearing, at the woman and her child, and he heard the iron of Rome in that mocking voice calling for him across the beach.

'Very well, Pwyllelni, Druid. Creep back into your hole. But, by Mithras! If you are taken up I shall swear that I've never clapped eyes on you – now silence for your life!'

The reins were harshly-dry under his fingers.

He gave them a pull and jerked the horse's head around.

'I'm here, you great dunderhead, my Pomponius! And I'll race you back and take two sestertii from you!'

FOUR

Isca – already being called Isca Silurum to distinguish it from
the old legionary fortress, now a civilian town hopefully awaiting the award of civitas capital when a forum might be built, of
Isca Dumnoniorum over the Strait to the south – lay waiting for
Marcus. The place had been meticulously laid out according to
the time-tested formula, and presented the reassuring turf-ram-
part walls, crowned with a palisade of stakes, the wooden
watch-towers, the four gates. Among the rows of leather tents
that of the legate lifted higher and more grandly. There was
where the Eagle was kept, with the cohors standards and the
trophies, the sacred vessels and the image of the emperor.

Yes! No doubt about it. The sight of the legions – their
camps, their fortresses, their standards, their leather tents –
lifted Marcus's heart. And nothing could so enthuse a man as
the eagle. The Eagle! By Mithras, many a man had willingly,
gladly, given his life to preserve that of the Eagle!

His father, who before his disgrace had been Legate of Legio
XX, had told him some yarns. Of men hacked to pieces still
stubbornly clinging to the Eagle, and striking about until they
were slaughtered and still refusing to part with the most
precious and sacred object known to a legionary. There had
been the tragic and disastrous affair of Varus – Varus! No one
liked to mention his name or that of his three doomed legions,
and they had never been re-created within the Roman Army.
The thought of three Eagles desecrated, contumed, blas-
phemed, somewhere out there in barbarous Germany filled any
man of the legions with a fury and a gloom and shivering dread.

Well, as Marcus well knew, if the men of Legio II Augusta,
here in Isca, had their say nothing so disastrous would befall
their Eagle. And the same went for the men of Legios VIIII,
XIIII and XX. By Mithras, the god of the Legions, yes!

There was a great deal of work to be done for the cohors
amicorum with Frontinus, and the new governor kept all his
people hard at it. Marcus found himself riding helter-skelter
about the country, carrying messages mostly, but often super-
vising the control of sudden small emergencies. Campaigning

weather would not last for ever, and everyone expected a massive attack on the Silures in their mountain strongholds.

Since the treacherous attack on him in Aquae Sulis, Marcus kept always on the alert. He had stumbled in with the javelin through his arm to make his report and they'd taken the thing out for him, not without a considerable amount of pain; but nothing had been found. In that brief interval between the pilum piercing his arm and the arrival of men with torches on the scene, the dead bodies had been removed.

Even the blood had been swept and covered with sand – but blood could not so easily be washed away, and Frontinus, grim with an unwanted worry along with the load of responsibility he bore, had been brusque.

'Yes, Britannicus. I agree you were attacked. But who by? And why? Until you can tell me that there is nothing I can do for you.'

'Yes, sir. I do not know who it was who sent the men, and I have no notion why anyone would wish to kill me.'

Frontinus, a hard man but a man with that jabbing sense of humour that so appalled non-Romans, said: 'The girl's brothers or father may give a reason, by Mars! You'd do well to tuck your tail into your clout henceforward, Britannicus.'

And so Marcus had been able only to say: 'Yes, sir,' and take himself off.

There was more to it than that.

A devil of a lot more.

One day, along with the most important force driving him on, he would find out.

A detachment of the Ninth marched in.

Marcus stood to watch them, moved as always by the sight of legionaries on the march. How these men could stride the world!

Even their forked sticks with their leather bags lashed into the fork, their messkit dangling about them, their easy relaxed air for all they marched at attention, wearing helmets, could not detract from their power. With iron and bronze, with bone and muscle and blood – and on their calloused feet – the men of the Legions had conquered the world – and were now about to finish off a little part remaining unconquered.

This vexillation comprised less than half the Legion, and the first cohort with the Eagle had not been included. The Legion's senior Tribune, a man readying himself for command of a legion in the near future, commanded the vexillation, which consisted of four cohorts. With them rode a young military tribune. Him – him Marcus watched with eyes that remained as flinty as one of these Silurian stream beds.

Publius Salvius, his name was.

Marcus had asked that immediately the detachment had come close enough for those tribunes of the Second with him to be able to pick out the faces of the coming Ninth.

Publius Salvius.

He would be number two.

He would have done to him what had been done to that bastard Gnaeus Paulinus in Rome.

But – this time far greater care must be taken.

Marcus felt the steel in him, harsh and unyielding, coiling ready to spring out with insane and murderous force.

'By the Names, my Julius! You look like a diseased camel about to give birth! Drink up and drown your ill-humour as only Bacchus knows how!'

Marcus roused himself. He had been lost in thought and the orgy had been going on for some time, and he supposed his face must have shown too much of his thoughts.

'I'll drink you flagon for flagon, my Pomponius! Aye, and sink you under the table—'

'What! With my belly! There's a score sestertes says you'll slumber first, my Julius!'

Marcus forced himself into the reckless laughter so common among these scions of the aristocracy of Rome.

'What! five denarii! My dear Pomponius – make each denarius a golden aureus and you're on!'

Pomponius roared his ready acceptance. Bronze or gold, it made little difference when their slave overseers might lash a little harder, or they might squeeze a banker that little bit more. Rome's wealth was so vast and it permeated down from the emperor to these bright young blades freely enough that nothing might be regarded as over-powerful. By the end of the night's drinking and debauchery a hundred, a thousand of those glittering golden coins might be wagered, and only roars of laughter greet the results.

Under the leather awnings of the tent, lifted up and joined so that a greater free space beneath could be obtained, the men of the governor's cohors amicorum as well as others of his aides prepared to rollick the night away. This might be their last chance for some time. No legionary would miss the chance of a last drink and debauch nor care over much about marching off to battle with a splitting headache and guts as yellowly-liverish as a sick dog.

Costly rugs strewed the floor, lamps in chains cast their golden light, carved-legged tables supported the food which the Romans knew so well how to procure at the far ends of the earth. So far the women had not been brought in. They would be saved for later. All was noisy good humour and uproar and eating and drinking. And, through it all as he and Pomponius prepared their wager, Marcus caught glimpses of the tribune of the Ninth, this certain Publius Salvius, as the fellow laughed and guzzled and drank and boasted.

In only a few years, Marcus supposed, instead of the Second living here in what was little more than a marching camp, they would have the comfort of stone walls and towers, of flagged courts and pavements, the praetorium would rise firm and solid at the centre, the granaries would be built of brick instead of wood. Yes, if Isca was to be settled as a Legionary Base, rather than a fort, as Frontinus probably intended, then the place would become a massive stone monument to the thoroughness and grandeur of Rome in the far corners of the world.

And, stuffed away somewhere in a putrescent hole, the carcase of Publius Salvius would quietly lie rotting away, to the bastard's eternal damnation.

Marcus watched the feasting with a cold and level gaze. He let himself shout out every now and then and he laughed with the rest; but all the time he was aware of how fragile was his control. He just wanted to stride over to Salvius and rip him up, serve him as Paulinus had been served.

If he did that he would be taken up at once and only an ignominious death could await him.

Marcus was not the same man who, a few years ago, would have risked that. He had learned a very great deal at Masada, and later, with old Linarius at the gladiatorial school run by that not particularly pleasant but undeniably efficient lanista. And the idea of failing now appalled him. For, and he knew this with the cold cunning of the serpent preparing to devour the rabbit, if he was not meticulously careful in his destruction of this Salvius, and as a consequence was taken up, then the others would escape. If he failed now, there would be no one else to exact the just vengeance.

Marcus Julius Britannicus was prepared to become cautious and cunning and devilishly vicious so as to bring eventual destruction upon all those who had ravished and slain his mother. He would not be content if a single one escaped.

These thoughts kept obtruding upon the thoughtless conviviality of the evening. He had continually to force the rigid muscles to relax, to iron out the harsh planes of mercilessness from his face, to smile and grimace, and to guffaw with the best of them.

His thoughts made him realize that merely to repeat what had happened to Paulinus would be to invite trouble, for the coincidences would be too great. No. No, he must try somehow to clamp down the anger and hatred in him, as the fires were clamped down within the Vesuvius above Pompeii, and so contrive a death for this Salvius that, awful and ghastly as it must of necessity be, would throw no suspicion back upon himself.

There had to be a way.

Marcus thought of his father. The old man had a way with him. He would have known what to do. Not for the first time Marcus wondered why his father had not given him his own name, as was so common and traditional among Roman patricians. How would he have felt had he been a Lucius instead of a Marcus? The old man must have had a reason. And Marcus knew without need for coherent thought that the reason had nothing to do with his father's marrying a British princess. The Iceni nobility were that, they were as royal as the old Tarquins – maybe that offended his father's old-time Republican principles, principles against which the emperors resolutely set their faces. If the Caesars could destroy the nobility of Rome they would do so. They had tried with venomous intent for a long time. But, in the end, the conspirators had got to his father, had disgraced him. Only in an honourable death had his father found honour.

No mercy for those who had done these things to his father and his mother entered Marcus's heart.

Salvius would be dealt with.

That remained as certain as the blood that flowed from the bull of Mithras.

'You are not keeping pace, Marcus!'

Marcus looked at Pomponius, flushed, lifting his goblet high, slopping wine down his already stained tunic. The lad was a good-enough intentioned idiot, a bit of a fool. He would merely serve out his time as a military tribune in order to qualify for the important posts of government later. He was no legionary. And now he was using Marcus's praenomen. Well, they were to be comrades for some time. It might serve. It might do very well.

Marcus would have need of friends. As a lonely man among patricians who knew of his origins and despised him for them, as a lonely man among patricians who did not know and shunned him for his reserve and coldness, as a lonely man among men, Marcus Britannicus knew little of friendship.

'I am two goblets before you – Caius.'

Pomponius blinked.

'By Mithras! Then I must make better speed.'

With that he tossed the wine down and slopped half of it over his chin, gobbling and choking, so that Nepos, fat face wobbling, shouted: 'Unfair! Unfair! The thumb for you, Caius!'

Caius Pomponius Endor hiccoughed, and wiped his lips, and roared for more wine, and the contest might go on.

Before long the shouts went up. Leading the clamour Publius Salvius roared his demands, banging a metal plate against the table to emphasize his words.

'Bring on the dancing girls!'

Finding girls in this outlandish spot at the edge of Empire who could dance had been a problem, and the six girls brought in did not promise much. Dancing and Romans had never been a happy combination, although Nero had shown what might be done. Marcus remembered the words of Cicero: 'Hardly anyone dances when sober – unless he is mad.'

So the men settled back, still drinking, to watch the dancing. They began to shout and boo and the girls, clearly frightened almost out of their wits, pranced about, waving their arms and their shawls, two of them with green-leaved boughs tracing patterns with them in the scented air.

The whole scene disgusted Marcus in a way he found too curious to bother to define. He liked watching girls dance. He liked to see their hips moving from side to side, so sensuously, so lithely, and to watch their breasts moving in sweet rhythm. He liked the sight of rosy limbs glowing through semi-transparent draperies. He liked very much the whole idea of all the warmth and passion of a girl's young body exhibited artistically and tastefully, not wantonly, although if the girl fancied doing that Marcus would not stop her. He seemed to see a greater dignity to a girl in thus dancing to her own bodily rhythms than any dignity a man might lose in salaciously watching her.

Salvius was not satisfied. He continued to bang his plate, keeping bad time, so that the flautists kept tangling their melodies, and the girls stumbled, losing their rhythm.

The noise grew. The scents became overpowering. Three or four of the young men had been sick all over the carpets, too lazy to go to the pit serving as a vomitorium outside. The uproar would be tolerated not only by Frontinus but by the Legate and the praefectus castrorum. The Legion was marching on the morrow and the young sparks must exorcise the demons in their blood.

The shrilling of the pipes grew as the flautists attempted to impose their patterns on the welter of noise. The girls spun and pirouetted and their shadows swirled across the tent. The glitter of wide-opened eyes, of teeth revealed behind laughing lips, of cup and goblet and platter, all shot sparks of fire into the scene. Most of the young men were good-naturedly clapping and yelling and urging the girls to even wilder prancing – Marcus watched Salvius sidelong and saw the fellow licking his lips, saw his flushed face and engorged cheeks, his hair sweat-slicked over his forehead, and his eyes, dark eyes protruding with lust and passion and arrogance.

He presented a picture so common as to be completely unremarkable.

The plate banging on the table annoyed Marcus.

The girls carried on with their dancing in a frenzy now, swaying and swinging, flinging their arms high, kicking their legs. Salvius bellowed along with the other tribunes and officers: 'Off! Off!'

Whether or not these local girls would resent this custom of Roman orgies Marcus did not know. He did not care, to be sure; but he watched Salvius.

A girl's drapery swirled into the air. Others followed. Bright eyes fastened upon slender bodies. If these girls were really only dancers they might very well be in for a harrowing time later on. The flutes screeched and piped, the draperies drifted into the air, falling like winged birds across the tables. Marcus shoved up from his elbow and brought his legs around under him. A bright saffron scarf floated past his head and he caught it, seeing the face of the girl who had thrown it off go swinging past above her last remaining veil.

'Off! Off!'

Marcus did not shout. He looked after the girl, saw her dark hair in its mass of ringlets, saw her slender body outlined and yet concealed by that last veil. He saw her hands – and realized her hands were trembling almost uncontrollably. Almost, for she could reach the fibula; but she could not press it, so great was the tremble in her limbs.

The girl stumbled, her rhythm destroyed. Her long legs flashed in the lamplight. There were cries and catcalls and obscene suggestions flying beneath the pressing roof of the tent. Salvius leaped from his table, shouting an oath, hurtling the plate away. He grappled with the girl.

'You silly useless bitch! I'll show you! Here – take it off – like this!'

And Salvius wrenched at the last remaining veil. The fibula held. The flimsy material ripped. The brooch, holding only long enough to start that tear, broke. The jagged edge drawn by the material down across the girl's breasts scored a long blood-red furrow in her skin. She screamed.

Salvius laughed and cuffed her across the face.

'Hold still, you stupid bitch! I'll show you how it's done in Rome!'

Marcus stood up. The girl, her young breasts firm and white, with that long obscene slash of blood down their round-ness, quivered in her terror as she shrank back. Her hair came free and swirled like a summer cloud about her burning face. Salvius roared his delight and seized her hair and so bore her back.

'I know all the tricks, drab! I'll show you things you've never dreamed of!'

His comrades were urging him on. Even Pomponius was cheering, waving his flagon; but Pomponius was well on the way to losing his wager and his golden aurei.

The girl's terror meant nothing to Marcus. Salvius – Marcus could see Salvius doing this in another place and another time. Out there as the military tribune dragged the girl's naked body to him, pressing his sweaty hands to her breasts, smearing the blood, grabbing her about the buttocks and heaving her up, out there a scene was being enacted that brought murder to

64

Marcus. He could not control himself. Gone was the cunning serpent; gone the sly cautious planning.

This whoreson out there! This bastard! This was one of the obscene fraternity who had— There was no feeling for the terrified naked girl in Marcus's heart. There was only room for hate.

He leaped the table. He landed lithely, balanced, and sprang forward. He took Salvius by the shoulder and swung him around and he struck the tribune across the face and he felt his fist smashed into flesh and bone and he struck again – and again—

Hands grasped him and hauled back and there were voices in his ears and hands dragging him back, and blood before his eyes . . .

Yes, very calm and cool and cunning, was Marcus Julius Britannicus.

'I will not accept an apology and I will kill the dog!' Publius Salvius gripped the arm of one of the tribunes, holding himself up, his face ghastly, blood from split lips and broken teeth fouling his mouth and dropping upon his tunic. 'The bastard won't get away with a reprimand from the governor! I'll smash him! I'll take his tripes out and – and—' He coughed and spat and the gob of blood hit the carpet by Marcus's feet.

They still held him. He had fought briefly like a wild animal. Then he had quietened. Now everyone waited. If the Legate got to hear of this, or the governor – but to Marcus's intense relief this animal Salvius was intent on having revenge in his own way. He wanted no official inquiry interfering with his intentions.

How well Marcus could understand that!

The tension of the moment remained in that lamplit tent with the cloying scents of wine and perfume mixed with the nauseous vomit upon the rugs. Slaves would be brought in to clean up – but first, first this matter of honour must be settled.

'But why, my Marcus?' demanded Pomponius, shocked back to semi-sobriety. 'Why, for the sweet name of Venus?'

'The man annoyed me,' said Marcus, and would say no more.

'The cestus?' suggested someone.

'Whips—' sang out another.

'Keep your voices down, and shout out only what sentries

65

might be expected to hear!' said Salvius, each word bringing a mass of blood to his lips. He took the proffered linen and wiped his face, cleansing himself in a bowl-tripod of warmed water. He had in a strange way taken command of the situation. Marcus was content to let the fellow do this; it made his own task easier.

'Not here,' said a tribune whose chin already showed blue, ready for the morning razor. 'And we have no amphitheatre here, yet.'

'In the woods. We are officers, tribunes. We can ride out and settle this thing.' Salvius looked up, the towel bloody in his fists. 'I wish to kill this dog – now!' He glared around, seeing the grim understanding on all their faces. No massive Roman law would satisfy Publius Salvius over this affront. He pointed at Marcus, his finger rock steady. 'And I choose the gladius!'

'But—' said Pomponius.

'I will fight you with whatever weapon you wish, you stinking bastard,' said Marcus, in a quiet, calm voice.

'Only one of us will return.' Salvius smiled, and winced, and touched the corner of his mouth. 'One only. The other will have been slain by the Silures, from ambush, and we will all be properly sorry and contrite for riding out so late – and the Legate will bellow at us, and I shall laugh, you diseased leper, when I think of the cur-dogs chewing on your bones.'

Marcus did not bother to reply. It was all arranged very quickly. Pomponius looked worried.

Marcus said: 'You perhaps think I have an unfair advantage, Caius?'

'It is not that, my Marcus. I wonder if I have the strength to mount a horse, and if I will fall off before we get where we are going. My guts feel like that damned ship off Dubris.'

And Marcus laughed.

He felt the strength in him. However it had happened, this would answer.

One of the tribunes came over, a young man with a face that looked too young for the grim work ahead, and yet he said: 'You would do well, Julius Britannicus, to choose some other weapon than a gladius. Salvius is – is known. He is deadly.'

'You would like to see him dead?' Marcus spoke bluntly.

That smooth young face flushed painfully. 'I transferred from the Ninth because of Salvius. The Second – I am happy here; and now he has turned up again.'

'I understand.'

'The cestus – I saw you strike him. But the gladius – he terrorizes the legionaries at drill – his skill—'

Pomponius hiccoughed and belched.

'I'll give you ten aurei on Marcus here, my lad, that is, if you care to back a man you hate so.'

'I would take your ten aurei, easily; but I will not wager on such as he.'

And the young tribune walked off, his head erect. Marcus looked after him. Then he turned away to prepare himself.

The young man's voice brought his head up. The tribune had halted, and half-turned. Everyone else had crowded out to see about the horses. Pomponius, Marcus and this young man were alone in the tent. The girls had been snatched away by their overseer, along with the flautists, long since.

'Marcus Britannicus—'

'Yes?'

'Should you by a miracle slay this Publius Salvius, and the story became known, you would do well never to go near Vellius Condorus.'

'I do not know him.'

'He is the friend of Salvius. The very dear friend. A powerful man. I tell you this out of hatred for Salvius and Condorus.'

'But no one will tell this Vellius Condorus. Will they?'

The silence was broken only by the fluttering of the lamps and the ever-present but muted distant noise of the camp and night stretched. Then the young man nodded his head, a little stiffly. 'You have the word of Valerius that I, at least, shall breathe no word of this.' He went out and the tent hanging fell into place. Pomponius opened his mouth to make the obvious comment when the tent flap lifted again and Nepos stuck his face in, all bulging cheeks and blazing eyes, to call: 'Marus Britannicus! All is ready. We await you.'

'I am ready, my Nepos.'

'And,' said Nepos, brilliant with excitement, 'Do not, for the sake of Mars and Venus, I beg you, my Julius, forget to bring your gladius.'

They rode out and through the thinned extensions of the woods, a bright careless company, full of laughter and ribaldry, whooping, joying in the thump of young blood through their bodies. Everyone could guess where they were going, and the sentries no doubt passed suitably acrid remarks about popinjay military tribunes, and time they learned what being a real legionary was all about. The natives of the land brought along, slaves almost without exception, had their habitations outside the legionary fortress. A small village nearby served as a convenient locale. All those grim legionary sentries walking the walls and standing watch in the towers knew the young bloods were off to find devilry and women and have themselves some fun. They'd face what the governor might say on the morrow – but, on the morrow, the legion marched.

A cleared space among the trees would serve.

Here the men dismounted and, being without slaves, had to tie their reins to tree branches themselves.

The leaves of the trees rustled and whispered secrets; but in the clearing the distant twinkle of stars, bright and hard in the velvet, gave little comfort. Their light was nowhere near sufficient and so the torches were brought and stuck in a ring. The tribunes and officers and aides clustered, wildly excited, the drink fuzzing their senses, their eyes coals of fire reflecting the torchlight dazzle. They were well away from observation here. Marcus took off his cloak and Pomponius held out his hand.

'Thank you, my Caius.'

Even Nepos was clustered about Salvius. Everyone gave him the right of the quarrel. Well, had there been nothing else hidden, dark and secret and bloody, beneath the surface, then Salvius would have had the right of it.

Any Roman who possessed Roman blood in his veins and a sure knowledge of how to quench his lust would make nothing of the foolish young dancing girl. That was what these inferior peoples existed for. No one would have given it a second thought. No one could understand what had come over Marcus Britannicus. But the tribunes of the Twentieth, informed by Valerius, late of the Ninth, knew of the reputation of Salvius as a swordsman. They were quite sure that justice would be done, and, into the bargain, this dark boor of a Britannicus would be put down at last and for ever – and about time too . . .

'Let us not waste time,' said Marcus. He spoke viciously. He wanted to feel his steel grate on bone, to feel the sweet sucking thrust as he struck through this bastard's saggy belly.

'I do not tarry, you dog!' Salvius swished his sword, striking

reflections of fire from the torches. The light, if erratic, was
ample to men accustomed to life with oil dips. 'Set yourself –
no apology can save you now!'

Marcus stepped forward.

'I am ready.'

Salvius smirked. He held out his hands and Marcus saw the
strength of them, and the unwavering blades, the points not
quivering by a fingernail rind. 'First your ears, Britannicus,
cur-dog. Then your lips – your nose – then I shall strike with
great pleasure lower—'

'Prattling bastard! Is your tongue your only weapon you dare
use?'

But no muscle moved that Salvius did not wish to move;
there came no angry reflex, no betraying spurt of rage. These
two could no longer incite anger; both were masters at that
game.

'Begin!' said a tribune of the Twentieth. His voice rasped,
hoarse and excited.

Salvius stepped back. Back . . . Marcus poised, watching,
ready to begin the deadly dance of steel. He saw Salvius circling, saw the sword in his right hand and the dagger in his left
abruptly sail up into the air, cross – and then Salvius charged in
with the gladius in his left hand and the pugio in his right.

Clever – clever!

The sword in his left hand darted for Marcus and the pugio
in his right, flashing across, grated on his sword and so drove it
up. Marcus brought his own dagger across with a convulsive
heave and leaped back.

'Ha!' shouted Salvius, and leaped back in his turn.

'By Mithras! You almost had him then, Salvius!'

Marcus said not a word. He knew about these fighters who
changed the weapons in their hands. He had seen knife-fighters
who advanced, smiling, throwing the knife from right to left
hand and back again, deadly, ominous, scarey to one who was at
a loss how to combat them . . .

In came Salvius, the two blades weaving, like the heads of
snakes drawn back ready for the strike.

Instantly, the moment he thought he had his man set, Salvius
went into a pass that should have ended up with Marcus's
left ear rolling on the grass and the side of his head spouting
blood.

The blades grated against one another, first gladius and

gladius and then dagger and dagger. Marcus twisted, brought his dagger back for that cunning cut to the inside of his opponent's arm, and Salvius, like quicksilver, eluded the cut and stabbed viciously. Marcus swayed, the blade passed his side, his return stab went nowhere, and then both men were apart and circling each other again, more wary, more conscious of the other's skills and strengths.

'Stick him, Salvius!' sang out a tribune.

'Let us see his tripes tangling around his knees!'

'Which ear is it first, then, my Publius? An aureus for the left!'

'Aye – and two for the right!'

The cries bounced like the ululations of bloodhounds around the clearing. Marcus debated. He could kill this bastard easily. Good as Salvius undoubtedly was, the man was no match for Marcus, trained as he had been in the hardest school of all. Against the gladiators Marcus had known and trained with, Salvius would have been coughing up his guts by this time. Unless the secutors decided that the crowd deserved a little entertainment, and then they might hold off and chop the tribune up, in much the same way he had boasted he would cripple Marcus.

So that was what he must do. He felt a regret that just vengeance should be perverted – but the thought of the remaining rapist-murderers drove him on.

The fight developed most interestingly. Soon the cat-calls from the watchers died away. No blood had yet been spilled. The combatants circled, and darted in, and thrust or cut, and leaped back. The blades rang or shrilled with that spine-tickling sound of sword against sword.

And now Marcus waited for each attack and each time he parried, and threatened a stab or a cut, and withheld the blow at the last moment, and so, gradually, he told Salvius with the utmost brutal savagery that the tribune's life was in his hands.

Publius Salvius understood this.

He saw more clearly with every pass that his best efforts were useless. He saw that he was a dead man.

Sweat slicked down his forehead. His mouth was open and he panted in hoarse hurtful gasps. Now his gladius trembled, the point making little circles in the air, the light runnelling the blade. He backed away, not caring to essay another attack.

'You bastard!' He panted the words, his chest heaving, the

sweat bright and shining like blood upon his forehead and cheeks. 'You filthy marsh-spawned worm – you cur-dog—'

Absolute silence clamped the ring of watchers.

Then: 'Stick the swine, Britannicus! Stick him!'

Valerius called, his youthful face ablaze with hate and a great and unholy joy, the greater because it had come so unexpectedly.

Marcus spoke.

'Oh, yes. I'll stick the miserable bastard. But not before he suffers – as others have suffered.'

And, there lay the flaw in his plans. He would not kill this animal until the animal knew why it was being slaughtered.

And it was exceedingly difficult to tell him with this ring of avid watchers about him – and kill him afterwards without the secret being revealed. Again, Marcus thought of those other men awaiting his just vengeance. He was not after revenge; he required justice and vengeance seen by himself to be justice.

In only the time it took for Marcus's gladius to beat aside Salvius's sword and poise for the next pass, Marcus had seen one answer to his dilemma. Instantly, acting on the thought, he swirled his blade, dazzled his dagger across Salvius's eyes and cut, neatly and precisely, with his sword, slicing Salvius's left ear away, so that it dropped limp and curled to the damp grass, and the blood glistened forth in a distended bubble, shining and reddish-black.

Salvius screamed.

The scream was echoed and a tribune span across the clearing, clutching his shoulder from which a spear protruded. A chorus of vicious yells burst about the Romans, and heavy bodies charged through between the trees. Pomponius yelled.

'Silures! We are ambushed! Fight – or we are all dead men!'

FIVE

The Silures were a tough independent folk, scratching a living on the higher slopes, concentrating their wealth and their power into the rich river valleys. They were not going to give up their lands and their lives without a struggle, and the chance afforded them of wiping out this parcel of young Romans was sent directly by Gwydion himself, the greatest of the Children of Don. That was as sure as the rainbow. They leaped howling across the clearing, hurling their spears.

Marcus cursed and beat away a flying spear with his sword.

'Into the trees!' a tribune was yelling.

A mad scramble followed as everyone broke for cover. The Silures followed, howling, their spears clattering into the tree trunks. Marcus did not stop to look at them. He ran. He picked up his feet and he ran.

The trees closed around him and he hunkered down beside a bush ready to despatch any painted savage who tried to kill him.

He was not prepared to sell his life dearly, as the poets sang.

He wanted to live. He had his just vengeance to follow and if he was dead then those bastard murderer-rapists of his mother would go free. He glared around with mad eyes. Where was Salvius?

A man wearing a chequered tunic ran past, a blanket rolled over his shoulder. He carried a spear and he poised ready to throw the instant he saw a target.

Marcus reached up and gripped the man's ankle and dragged him down. The pugio kissed across the neck and the blood poured out and one Silurian mother would weep for a son.

The Silurian had a swarthy face, much darker than those of the Belgae or the Iceni, and his hair was dark and extremely curly. Marcus bundled him further under the bush and stared about for the next person to taste his steel.

A great deal of yelling and shouting was going on, and the noise of tree branches thrashing. A man shrieked; but the language was not comprehensible through the agony.

With this amount of noise the sentries would be alerted and a party of legionaries would come running out. They might be as many as a double-century from the guard details, and this maniple would deal most effectively with the Silures. Marcus meant to remain alive until then. He saw this as a sacred duty to the memory of his mother.

There were three maniples with their hand-crowned standards to a cohort, and the fifth cohort, because they were not going marching out on the morrow, were on guard duty this night.

Marcus peered about warily in the night. The ring of torches still burned in the clearing. By their light he could see the writhing shadows and determine if the blackness was mere shadow of tree and branch, or the dark intent form of a man creeping to slay him.

There was every chance that before the legionaries arrived a detachment from the auxiliaries would come storming in, thirsting, as always, to prove they were as good as the legions. There was a cohort of Syrian bowmen to hand, and an ala of cavalry – the First Thracians – to back them if necessary.

Through the streaming erratic light of the torches Marcus saw the lump of solid shadow at the foot of a tree stir and move. He waited. The shadow extended an arm, and torchlight glittered from a blade. The shadowed mass moved on, the star-glitter from the sword was quenched, and the shadow humped further into the trees.

Marcus looked about. He could see no one and the noise was racketting away from him. Only a wounded man would crawl along like that. Marcus stood up. With his gladius held poised and ready before him he walked silently over to stand above the mewling, sobbing, creeping form of Publius Salvius.

Trumpets sounded, shrill and yelping, through the darkness where the trees swayed their dark branches in traceries against the stars and the night breeze whispered in the leaves.

'Before I kill you, Publius Salvius, it is necessary for you to know why you are going to die.'

The tribune hoisted himself up on a knee, his hand clawing up the rough bark of the tree. His face, clearly visible in the fleering lights of the torches, turned up and showed a mere pale splodge, studded with the pits of eyes and mouth and the sucked hollows of cheeks. Blood from the site of his missing ear swelled black and festering.

'Kill me? Not now – the savages, the painted barbarians–'

Marcus felt the beginnings of the peace he craved trembling over him. This fool thought that their quarrel could be forgotten in face of a greater danger, assumed that an attack by the Silurian savages would unite them against a common foe. Well, that might have been so, had the quarrel been merely what Salvius thought it to be.

Marcus intended to disabuse him of his misconception.

Then he'd destroy the bastard.

One of the heavy British spears had pierced through Salvius's calf, dragging him down, forcing him to crawl. Marcus seized the haft and twisted it up and Salvius screeched in agony.

'You dog, Britannicus! Our quarrel means nothing now! We must warn the fort – get the legion out – these painted savages threaten the men of Rome–'

'You are going to die, Salvius. And you must know why you are going to die so unpleasantly.'

Salvius looked into Marcus's eyes, the long shuddering look of a man staring upon doom. Torchlight struck red madness in Marcus's eyes. Salvius recoiled.

'You're mad! Insane!' He lifted his voice, shouting with frenzied desperation, almost incoherent with shattering fear.

'If you shout you will bring the Silures.'

And Marcus slapped his face, four times, back and forth.

For a space Marcus was content merely to stand looking down on Salvius. The man's gladius was kicked away out of reach, his pugio had long since been dropped. Just why he stood and watched, Marcus could not say. Was it merely that he gloated? Did he just gloat over his victim? Or were the deeper feelings of disgust and repugnance at soiling his hands on this vermin making him draw back?

With a snarl as savage as a cave lion of Syria, Marcus drew back his foot and drove his iron-hard toes into Salvius's side. The man screeched and flopped about, and twice more Marcus kicked him. He bent.

He seized the wretch's hair and twisted him up so that his mad face glared down insanely into the white upturned face of the other. There was no reluctance to soil his hands now, no, by Mithras! He wanted to sink his fingers in this bastard's eyeballs. He wanted to rip out his tongue – He spat full into the tribune's face.

'Listen, you sack of vomit taken from the triclinium – you heap of dung shovelled on to the dungcarts – I will tell you why I am going to kill you. You will not die easily, you will die in agony, shrieking – except that your tongue will be ripped out – and I shall laugh, Salvius, laugh at your torment!'

'You are mad—'

'Yes. Of course—' and then, speaking in a voice that began low and hoarse and rose until the hoarseness turned into a maniacal shriek, Marcus told Publius Salvius why he was going to die in torment.

Before he had finished Salvius was wailing and sobbing and trying to crawl away. Casually, in mid-sentence, Marcus swung the gladius and chopped through Salvius's ankle. The foot in its elegant evening sandal flopped away into the damp grass. Marcus continued speaking as though no interruption had occurred.

'Think about these things, Salvius, and shudder and shriek, and no remorse can save you now – none – no power on this earth can save you now, you whoreson.'

'But we were drunk—' Salvius tried to hold his shattered ankle and in the torchlight his fingers showed a stream of black liquid, shot through with red, glistening and streaming. 'There was no force – it was afterwards—'

The fellow had courage. He was arguing for his life. He must see that Marcus was crazed. His kind would do any cruel and arrogant deed and then, given the chance, argue their way out of payment. They knew the whole world owed them a living. But, just because Salvius was courageous, just because he could face up to what was happening, at the end, could not stop Marcus.

'What do you mean – afterwards?'

'After they had enjoyed her, then she was forced to speak of the treasure.'

'Treasure?'

'Much treasure – she was made to talk – I – it was not me—'

Marcus shook him. His face in the torchlight was turning green, like a piece of cheese floating on a cloaca. Salvius's head lolled back, and he gargled an exhausted breath, clogging in his chest.

'You bastard!' said Marcus. 'You're not going to die on me!'

'No – no—' shrieked Salvius, then; but the strong and agile fingers of Marcus Julius Britannicus were quickly at work preventing any further outcry.

He wasn't having this fellow die peacefully on him before he had taken his vengeance.

'Look on me, Salvius, for the last time. I am the son whose mother you raped and tortured and slew. Now you will pay for your crime—'

And so the darkness descended for Publius Salvius.

Marcus served him as Gnaeus Flavius Paulinus had been served back in Rome.

'And do you, too, boast that you are descended from Venus, my Julius?'

'Only if the girl proves reluctant, my Caius.'

'Ha! Then you never cease prattling of your divine ancestor!'

At that moment Pomponius's horse shied at a jackdaw fluttering from the rocks, and he clung on, cursing and flapping with his whip. Marcus laughed. Yes, he could laugh again, now. Since the night when the foolish tribunes had been surprised and attacked in the forest, the night which had seen, among other dead, the death of Publius Salvius, he had felt in excellent spirits. Two gone. Four more to go – and Crassus, luxuriating in Pompeii.

Now the army marched north up the river deep into the country of the Silures. This was an army marching ready for instant attack, and so the familiar marching pattern of the army when in less hostile country had been slightly altered. The surveying team with their instruments marched at a safer position. Up ahead went the mounted auxiliaries, and then the foot auxiliaries, with a strong detachment of the legion to provide a powerful buffer force to take the initial attack and act as the legion's shield. Around that forward detachment the auxiliaries could manoeuvre, and to it the rest of the legion, with the vexillation of the Ninth, could hasten to smash the attack from the flank and rear. Iron men in iron corselets, with iron weapons in their hands, the men of the legion marched. Not for nothing were they given the nickname derived from their caligae, their hob-nailed boots. The foot-sloggers. The men who carried the Eagles to the far corners of Empire, who marched past the frontiers, who formed the iron core of the army.

Mist clung about the mountains to either hand. Away over there eagles and hawks spiralled in the air, always seeking for prey. How apt it was and right that the men of Rome marched with their Eagle standard into battle! The aquilifer held as proud a position as any man dared hoped for who joined the legions at eighteen and worked and trained and sweated and made his way up the ladder of promotion so laboriously. A clever man, the aquilifer. The Eagle rode high above the helmets of the marching ranks, and ever and anon a sun-glint struck from it, slicing through the misty atmosphere, and a man's heart would lift at the sight.

A horseman galloped back along the flank of the marching lines, his horse lavishly decorated with bronze ornaments, his uniform a blaze of bronze and red. Pomponius sniffed.

'Showing off again – Licinius will do himself a mischief if he thinks to impress a patrician.'

Marcus glanced at the oncoming military tribune of the Second. This Licinius was one of the five tribuni augusticlavii, and although it was usual for these men working their way up to be a little older than the general idea of a feckless young tribune, Licinius would have to be very careful that old age did not overtake him before he finished his three periods of militiae. To join the ranks of the Equestrians it was absolutely necessary to own capital at least to the value of 400,000 sestertii, so Licinius was not a poor man.

'Keep the men moving there!' he bellowed as he pranced along. He looked splendid, no doubt of it.

Seeing Marcus and Pomponius he reined across, with much pirouetting and curvetting from his mount, and fell in beside them.

'Well, my Licinius,' said Pomponius, the irony in his voice lost on the tribune. 'And is the legion up to your satisfaction?'

'When I commanded my cohors of Batavians we showed what marching was!'

Marcus lifted an eyebrow. But he let it pass. The fool bragged of his cohors of auxiliaries. Well, even Marcus could see that a man who wanted Equestrian rank and must serve his three periods of military duty – the first as commander of a cohors of auxiliary infantry, the second as a military tribune with a legion, the last as a prefect of a cavalry ala – would wish to make as much as justly he could from his auxiliaries.

77

Marcus, for one, along with thousands of others, welcomed the work done by this non-citizen force for the legions.

And, too, as Marcus watched Licinius whip up his horse and gallop dramatically off, already shouting, the very fact that the man could show these feelings about his men must weigh in his favour. After all, he was doing his tres militiae with the fighting men only so that he might gain a coveted position later on – a procurator of importance, say, or any of the many and complex positions open to the Equestrians. For everyone except the centurions and the legionaries, the army was merely one, sometimes tedious, step on the way of a brilliant career.

The legion marched and the mist clung and the distant tree-clad hills paralleled their course up the valley. Marcus turned in his saddle and looked back. The unrolling carpet of men streamed on behind, and when he looked forward the image was reversed, as though he looked into a trick mirror. Frontinus would call his aides when they were wanted; for now there was little for them to do on this particular part of the march.

So Marcus reflected on this Licinius and his behaviour. He had spoken fair to Pomponius – he had ignored Marcus Britannicus.

Not for the first time Marcus found himself up against this wall of aristocratic snobbery, this sneering contempt of him and his origins. These men could not understand why he had acted towards Salvius as he had, and the attack of the Silures, although it had covered the traces of Marcus's handiwork, had not washed away the memories of what had happened in the tent from these men's hearts. As he had in Judaea with Silva, so here in Britain with Frontinus, Marcus would smash anyone and anything who sought to drag him down. Now, he had further and more pressing reasons to continue. There were four of the whoresons left – and Crassus.

'You look just like the sharpening stone, my Marcus! I swear by Venus a green legionary will sharpen up his gladius against your nose and chin!'

Marcus roused himself and looked across at this Pomponius, this reckless, lazy, careless young man masquerading as an officer of the legion acting as equerry to the governor.

'Why, my Caius, do you continue to speak to me, to ride with me – why, even our fat friend Nepos avoids my look.'

'As to that, my Marcus—' And Pomponius averted his own eyes, and hawked and spat – most accurately at a little lizard running under a rock at the side of the trail – and said: 'By Mithras, I do not know! You are as cross-grained as a twisted timber in the stockade. Yet I would not – By the stinking bowels of Vulcan, my Marcus – I do not know!'

And Marcus Julius Britannicus laughed.

He threw back his head, and he laughed, and so, looking up against the misty dazzlement of the sky, saw the incoming spears like flecks of dark paint against the grey.

The trail wound through a low pass, a pass that should have been cleared by the cavalry. And the Silures had crept back and were up there hurling down spears! And the auxiliary infantry were opening out and their shields were coming down into line and they were racing up the grassy slopes of the hill, racing to cut off the Silures before they could leap back on to their chariots.

Men yelled and trumpets blew. The great slogging mass of the legion merely assumed – suddenly, suddenly! – a different appearance as every shield clicked into lock and like a serpentine testudo the legion tramped on. Not for them this scurrying about over hillsides chasing painted savages! Not for the iron men of the legions this skirmishing with charioteers.

'By Mithras, Marcus! Here is sport!' And with a wild whoop Pomponius lashed up his horse and went bounding away across the slope to join with the auxiliaries. With a ferocious curse, Marcus prodded Pluto and the big black lunged forward.

He could see the small active figures of the Britons ahead. As the original intention had been to draw a body of troops out, that purpose had been achieved. Now the more traditional slingers stepped forward into action.

The Iceni, his mother's people, were fair or red-haired, light-complexioned, and although they too fought with chariots, they were not the famous slingers of Britain. These men up ahead were. Their sea-washed pebbles could crack a man's head open. The slingers employed by the Roman army used lead bullets, cunning lozenge-shaped missiles with a much greater range than the pebbles of the Silures; but Marcus knew that if a British-slung pebble struck him on the head, helmet or no helmet, he'd have a damned great head-ache if he was lucky. If he was not lucky his brains would gush out through his nostrils and ears.

He jammed in his heels and drew his sword and went haring up along the slope after Pomponius.

The auxiliaries had their shields well up. Pebbles rattled against the wood like hail. The line did not waver. The mist curled ahead, and the grassy slope that had looked so gentle and unmenacing from below quickly became steeper than one expected and the grass, slippery in the wet, treacherous underfoot. The auxiliaries panted on and Pomponius was past their flank and whooping into the first of the Silures.

Short, dark, curly-haired men, stripped to the waist, wearing chequered trousers, the Silures howled and slung – and the pebbles clattered against shield and helmet and sang sizzling through the air.

Marcus stuck his head down and went on, just peering from under the brim of his helmet. He was wearing a tolerably smart bronze breastplate, only lightly sculpted with the outlines of muscles – the really ornate breastplates were the prerogative of the higher ranks – and he had some confidence in his helmet; but a smack from a slung stone, from a British sling ... He went on, Pluto's hooves thudding on the turf, steam jetting from his nostrils, going up and down, surging on full of muscle and fire and power.

Men were reeling from the line. The yelling, although thin and attenuated, still held that shrilling ring of fierce ardour, clear and imperious. Pluto's hooves battered the turf. A centurion staggered, flinging up his arms, his vine stick catapulting into the air. His white cloak billowed like a shroud as he fell. The men yelled, deep and angry, and the auxiliaries charged.

At that instant, as the spears flew and the lines rushed forward, Marcus rounded the end to come up with Pomponius and saw his horse pitch over, to roll and kick, to shudder and to lie still. Probably two or three pebbles had struck the beast on the head simultaneously. Pomponius was thrown clear. He was on his feet, his gladius in his hand, drawing his cloak up around his left arm. He might curse the army and never wish to know what being a legionary was – but he prided himself on his swordsmanship.

Now he would be tested.

'Hold, my Caius!' bellowed Marcus. 'Hold!'

The wild men surrounded him, and spears stabbed in, a mass of naked backs and chequered trousers obscuring Marcus's view of the scene, all a swirl of skirling madness.

Marcus, bent over his horse's head, had to shout louder than usual. 'Come on, boy! Come, Pluto, my beautiful! Straight into them and use your hooves! At them Pluto!'

The big black responded to the voice and to the familiar commanding pressure of thighs and knees, the thump of heels into flank. He bounded forward and, in the instant before he reared up, he neighed wildly, his teeth glinting, his nostrils red as fire, spurting steam. His forelegs lashed out and his hooves crushed the skull of the nearest Silure. The man's head caved in and he fell like a rag doll.

Marcus leaned down, sweeping with his sword in the prescribed fashion. The gladius might be designed for thrusting; it happened to be a perfectly balanced weapon for cutting. In vicious slashes and cuts Marcus hacked a way forward. Pomponius, streaming blood, still stood. Half a dozen Silurians lay about him.

'By the belly and breasts of Venus, my Marcus! You are welcome!'

'Up, my Caius! Mount!'

Pluto pirouetted, span, Pomponius leaped. Marcus got his left arm around the equerry, hoicked him up, leaned to avoid a spear thrust and smashed his sword down in a bloody arc. Pluto neighed fiercely. A spear gashed his glossy black flank. Marcus cursed and back-handed the spearman, taking away his nose and half his face. The blood smoked into the misty air.

Then a familiar shield with the Roman markings bashed into the next spearman and a gladius did its work, and then another shield and another gladius popped into line alongside the first, and the auxiliaries had arrived and were methodically butchering all those Silurians who did not have the sense to run.

Pluto carried Marcus and Pomponius away angling down the little hill. At the bottom, with the iron ranks of the legion passing, they looked up. The hill looked ridiculously small and low to have afforded cover for such an encounter.

'The cavalry will catch it in the neck.' Pomponius spoke feelingly. 'And I need a horse.'

'Pluto can carry two until tonight.'

Pomponius spat and both men dismounted. They stood for a moment, whilst Pomponius cleared his mouth of the blood.

'A glancing blow from one of these devilish pebbles.'

'You placed your head in range.'

'Aye! I know! I wanted to get a whack in—' Pomponius

laughed and twisted his face up, and fingered his mouth gingerly. 'Damned pebble! When I laugh my mouth—'

'Then to stop you from laughing I suggest you contemplate what Frontinus will say to you. What duty has an equerry to go chasing off into a fight with the auxilia?'

'None, I grant you, my Marcus. But it warmed the blood in this damp climate.' Pomponius suddenly looked solemn. He held out his hand. 'Thank you, Julius Britannicus. I give you my thanks for my life.'

'The gift was not mine to give, Caius, only yours to throw away.'

'Um,' said Pomponius. 'You do not spare a fellow, do you!'

Within the context of Frontinus's strategy in invading the domains of the Silures by sea-borne invasions and advances up the river valleys, the skirmish found no mention, not even a footnote in the official records. But men were dead. A centurion, attached from the legions to the auxilia, was dead, his white cloak dappled with blood, his vine stick broken, the phalerae upon his chest meaningless lumps of metal.

The advance would go on. Frontinus had negatived the idea of a simple and brutal attack due west, into the mountains. This isolated country far on the west of Britain, with its mountains and valleys, had resisted stoutly. There were many young men of the tribes anxious to test the mettle of Rome, forgetful of the experiences of their fathers at the hands of the men of iron. Frontinus left-hooked his way along the south coast, and every time the Romans landed and marched inland they built a camp-fortress, and garrisoned it, and marched on, and so denied more and more land to the Silures.

Once the Silures had been crushed, then it would be the turn of the Ordovices. Roman might made manifest by her army could not be stayed by half-naked savages with pebble-slings, with spears, and with long swords that bent in battle.

As always, once the day's march had been completed and the camp had been set up and sentries posted and the cooking fires burning merrily to cook the men's porridge, so then Marcus would be hard at it, flinging Pluto into his racing stride, carrying messages, seeing that orders had been carried out, doing all the hundred and one things an aide of the cohors amicorum had come to this outpost of Empire to perform.

That his primary function when he had joined Frontinus was to act as a scout seemed to have been forgotten.

There were few opportunities for the leisurely dinner parties so beloved by the upper classes, and bathing became a strictly functional part of campaigning. No wonder the Romans bemoaned campaigning!

Licinius, the military tribune of the Second serving his second military service period, had a toothache, and went around asking people for the best remedy. Among all the serious suggestions made, quoted by the most eminent authorities in Rome, like cooking a black chameleon or rubbing a rabbit's brains on the gums, Marcus slyly said: 'I heard a doctor in Herculaneum claims veritable miracles for his latest cure.'

'Yes, yes!' demanded Licinius, holding his jaw, his face contorted. 'Tell me, Britannicus, for the love of Venus.'

They were walking back from the latrines, where a pleasant time had been spent, and the night sky showed starless and dank, clouds high and invisible and shutting out that distant glitter of starlight.

Fat Nepos said something in a low voice; but Licinius shrugged him off.

'My tooth is killing me, Nepos! I wouldn't care if he was painted blue all over!'

Marcus's face remained iron hard. He said: 'This man – and I only repeat his words, I cannot vouch for the cure, since Mithras has seen fit to bless me with strong white teeth – has said that if you collect a donkey's dung, boil it up in a copper pot with the urine of a horse, and then evaporate the result into a paste and smear the paste liberally on the teeth—'

'By Mars! That sounds powerful!'

'Oh, yes, the stronger the better. Over all the teeth and gums, the doctor said – he was a Greek, a little wizened fellow.'

'They are skilled, the Greeks, no doubt of that.'

'Yes, indeed. Strong dung, strong urine, and plenty of it well rubbed in.' Marcus paused, said: 'Of course, he did say—' and paused again.

'Yes, yes?' Licinius twisted his face around, his eyeballs rolling, glistening in the gleam from a watchfire. 'Yes, what more?'

'Only that if the dung and urine were blessed by a follower of Isis, the effect would be greater. You might then dispense with the boiling, and simply mix them together, the stronger the better, and apply them directly. A good mouthful, the doctor said, liberal, liberal—'

'Isis! There is one – in the Eight Cohort! At least one – they are a sly lot in the Eighth! I'll to him directly, my slaves can collect—' His voice drifted into the darkness as he hurried off, limping with the pain in his tooth.

Pomponius belched and guffawed and started: 'By the Names, Marcus! That—'

And Marcus cut him off with: 'Dice tonight, my Caius? Or is it—'

'Dice it is, my Marcus. Nepos – you will—?'

But Nepos, shaking his fat face, took himself off. He said, softly: 'Herculaneum? A Greek from Herculaneum? That takes a power of belief, even for a man with a toothache.'

'A man with a toothache will believe anything,' said Marcus. And then – and only then – he laughed.

Marcus and Pomponius were about to settle to their dice when an orderly appeared, stiff in the lamplight, to summon Marcus to the governor's tent. Pomponius yawned.

'Sooner you than me, this time of night! By the backside of Venus! I am tired – I am obliged to the governor. He has relieved me of relieving you of your aurei.'

'Save your purse until tomorrow, my Caius. I will have it then.' As he spoke Marcus was rapidly strapping back on his equipment, for he guessed a night ride lay ahead. The money given him by the husband of Agrippina for the successful fight against the enormous black gladiator Atilus had lasted well; but life among the brilliant blades around the governor made deep inroads on his purse. Whatever the governor wanted, it had deprived Marcus of the chance to build up his reserves.

What Frontinus wanted was not what Marcus expected.

The pro praetor's tent showed all the luxurious living expected of a Roman governor of a province, even on campaign. But that luxury was contained and held within the iron grip of a man with a mission in life. As of now, that task was to crush the Silures, and then probably the Ordovices, so that they might not attack the environs of Roman power. But that immediate aim was merely the continuing process which had brought Frontinus through the necessary positions he had held to his current post of Governor of Britain. Soon, with that job safely behind him he could go on to greater things, such as the pro-consulship of one of the rich and harvest-worthy provinces of Asia. Britain was very high in the list of appointments, but once a man had attained that eminence, it would be rare if his ambition would not fire him to finish the course.

'Ah, Britannicus. You will drink a cup of wine with me as I tell you what you are going to do.'

'Yes, sir, thank you, sir.'

A freedman with ink smudges on his fingers and an indelible ink smudge behind his ear sat to one side ready to write down the orders Frontinus would give, so that Marcus would have no excuse for failure to understand at any later date.

'We are out here on the frontier, Britannicus, doing what has to be done. We thought Suetonius had destroyed the Druid power in Mona. But he did not. What I am telling you now is confidential – d'you understand that?'

'Yes, sir.'

'H'mmph.' Frontinus scratched his head, where his hair, combed forward and trimmed into neat locks in the fashion, made him look younger than the solid lines and the thickness of his neck indicated he really was. He wore a tunic; a toga would be out of place here and his uniform would be in the hands of his slaves, being polished to a mirror brightness. 'You are going south across the strait – a ship is waiting in the river mouth. You carry a message to Publius Popilius Pothinus, commanding a vexillation of the Ninth at Doninna. The Twentieth are advancing westwards up the river from Viroconium Cornoviorum. Since the Fourteenth Gemina were misplaced in their loyalties in the year of troubles, and although returning to Britain have now been sent, it seems permanently, to Germany, we are without their dash and experience. And the Second Adiutrix have their hands full.' Frontinus sipped his wine, and stared thoughtfully at Marcus. 'I particularly wish to relieve the military of the necessity of garrisoning forts in areas where the natives have been pacified and are ready, indeed looking for and welcoming, the provision of Roman civitas. One day, perhaps, the citizenship will be extended to them, but that is not for now. They must become civilian towns and learn to take care of themselves.'

Well, that was the usual way of it with Rome. Once an area had been cleared of disaffection and the legions had moved on then the people must learn to ape the ways of their betters in the Eternal City. Marcus could feel the pebble slung on its cord around his neck pressing into his chest. A worthless little pebble, of no value; yet it had been given him when he was a young boy by Queen Boudicca herself; worthless it yet held an incalculable value for him.

He waited whilst Frontinus drank more wine, and stared for a space into the lamp-shrouded shadows of the tent. At last Frontinus said: 'The Druids are stirring up trouble again. I will not tolerate this. The thought of their practices makes the gorge rise; yet it is not the ethical question that poses the most serious problems.'

'I see that, sir,' ventured Marcus. He had no wish to appear a wooden dummy like the stakes against which the green legionaries practised their swordsmanship; yet he had no wish to appear forward.

'Yes. I had a high regard for your father, Britannicus. There were those who – well, it is a long time ago, now. We must look to the power of Rome. If the tribes are roused and come out against us, and we tangled in these Mars-forsaken Silurian hills—'

The prospects were those to make a military man sweat.

The legions were committed, the Twentieth Valeria Victrix – his father's old legion – coming in from the north, the Second Augusta here in the south. The Second Adiutrix were busy, as Frontinus had said, and only a handy vexillation of the Ninth Hispana from Eboracum was available so far down into the south, ready to strike into the land of the Dumnonii. From Lindinis they could march westwards and Frontinus indicated that reports suggested the Durotiges would not rise.

'Only the fools who do not see the truth will take to arms, Britannicus. The Druids are maleficent. They arouse the young men, inflame with wild words, send them off to be killed. It will be bad business if Pothinus cannot interpose himself. There is no time to be lost. You will carry my orders directly and deliver them in person. Is that understood.'

Marcus fisted his chest. 'It is understood, sir.'

Frontinus bent to his work table and picked up a letter the seals of which had been so savagely broken they had splintered. The scroll had been tightly rolled and he ripped a portion loose as he flattened it. He scarcely glanced at it before lifting his eyes to Marcus. The governor looked a bitter man.

'It is the same old story. The Dumnonii objected to being

taxed. By Mithras! Don't they know that is what they were born for? The sub-procurator writes they burned the wagons taking the corn, broke the amphorae of oil – he is doing what he can. You must report the exact circumstances to me, Britannicus. The emperor will hear of this, nothing escapes him. I want to know why the sub-procurator had this trouble – you will see him, this Vellius Condorus. Now, Britannicus, let Mercury speed your heels.'

Vellius Condorus!

The friend of Publius Salvius!

And – with this detachment of the Ninth there might be one of the remaining murderer-rapists. Not might! There *would* be!

The orders from the governor he carried could not make him travel faster than the hungry desires of his own heart.

SIX

Rain beat mercilessly down and the track splashed into a stream of liquid mud. The horses plodded miserably. Marcus had been unable to bring Pluto, and had with considerable misgivings entrusted the big black to the care of Pomponius Endor. Pomponius had been ablaze with the idea of going off on a secret mission; he had had to be content with a magnificent black stallion. Marcus heartily wished he rode Pluto now; the nag under him slipped and stumbled, a skinny scrawny pony used to half-naked barbarians and not an armoured man of Rome.

When Marcus's great-uncle, Publius Petronius Turpilianus, had laid down the consulship in the eight hundred and fourteenth year of the city he had come to Britain as governor. Well, the old boy had done the sort of job the task required at the time, a policy of peace and conciliation after the violence. Those hawk-like writers of Roman society might comment acridly on Turpilianus's lack of military effort; the happy results of his work, carried on by his successor, Trebellius Maximus, had borne fruit. The whole southern part of the country was now peaceful. In fact, the famous Legio XIIII Gemina had been sent off to the east. Now the blood-lust had been aroused again in the peaceful men of the southwest. What the end would be no one could say, except that Rome would triumph.

The small force of auxiliary cavalry with him, a half turma of Spanish horsemen, bore looks of disgruntled hatred for the weather. Time had rushed by this year, already it was two days before the nonae of November. The weather had broken and travel was so atrocious as to be impossible except for well-mounted men determined to push on regardless of the cost.

The decurion commanding the cavalry, a rough-tongued individual with a face scarred from some old battle and eyes so black they might have been cut from the hide of a Nubian, reined up, pointing ahead. Through the slanting spears of rain a sodden village showed, turf huts, low-thatched, their doors closed and no smoke to be seen. Split-paling fences contained half a dozen ponies, shag-headed beasts with mangy sides and bushy tails, huddled against the rain.

'New mounts!' said the Spaniard. 'If any man's horse fails him, he'll have to ape the caligatae and walk.'

The cavalrymen rode up and no time was lost in knocking away the palings and rounding up the horses. The beasts were in better shape than those under the Romans; but there was little to choose in it.

The horses neighed, pawing the air, frightened.

A house door jerked, then creaked and opened stiffly on its wooden pegs. A shock of hair shoved out into the rain and before the man stood up he was bellowing: 'Get away from those horses, you heap of dung, Gwanlion! I've told you before—'

Only Marcus could understand the Celtish. The man straightened, bulky in chequered trousers with an old cloak, brown and threadbare with age, pulled over his head. He saw the riders. His mouth closed, his face, already streaming water, blanked.

'Hurry it up,' the decurion was snarling, savaging his horse around, dismounting in a flurry of wringing wet cloak. The Spaniards were busily changing saddles, and a brisk argument developed among them as to who of the sixteen men of the turma should take a fresh mount. The Celt finished gaping and waddled forward, waving his arms.

His shouts and protests elicited nothing beyond a curse from the Spaniards.

Marcus said: 'We merely change horses. I think you will get the better of the bargain.'

The man stared up, the water dripping from his beard, his eyelids half closed. He understood what was happening. He shook his head, and mumbled, low in his beard, and whatever it was he said Marcus, for one, had no wish to hear it.

'Your horse, sir,' and Marcus turned to feel the reins thrust into his hand. He and the decurion would take two of the new mounts, the rest would go by seniority or by right of fist.

Mounted up, Marcus turned the horse's head and heard a frenzied yell. The Celt ran towards him, flinging up his arms, bellowing, and then pointing to the cavalrymen. Marcus stared. The Spaniards had taken the man's horses; but they had not left their own. These, riderless, trailed on after the rest, a tiny remuda that meant livelihood to the Celt.

'You said!' he screamed. 'Master! You told me—'

'Decurion!' said Marcus. This whole affair disgusted him with its pettiness, a squalid incident in the mud and rain. 'Why are you not leaving the exchange horses?'

The decurion sidled his horse over. His dark face with the water drops upon it showed the fierce satisfaction of a military mind making a vital decision.

'We shall need to travel fast, sir. The spare horses can be ridden turn and turn about. We'll travel faster that way.'

That was true.

'Your horses are being requisitioned in the name of Rome,' he told the Celt. He spoke with the habitual harshness of a legionary explaining self-evident truths to idiots.

The Celt shrieked. He knew as well as anyone that he'd never see the horses again. He flew at Marcus, his hands raised, and this time with menace. A knife glinted, runnelled with water. 'Roman lap-dog! You will not steal from an honest man again—'

Marcus watched him, poised, ready on the horse. The decurion whipped out his sword and brought the flat down hard on the Celt's head. The man pitched head first into the mud. The knife flew through the rain. Some of the cavalry guffawed.

The decurion looked at Marcus. 'He ought to be chopped, out of hand. I've a mind to give it to him—'

A woman appeared at the house doorway, and other faces showed from the other miserable hovels. Marcus felt the tiredness lapping him in fatigue and a despair he had no right to allow.

'No, decurion. Do not kill him. Let him lie.'

'If you say so, sir.'

This man was not a legionary, for there were no decurions in the legions; but he had been trained up well. If his officer gave him an order he would obey. But Marcus did not miss the elaborate way the Spaniard spun his sword, catching it by the hilt, before sheathing it back in the scabbard. The young officer was squeamish about shedding blood . . .

Patiently, Marcus said: 'There is a potential insurrection near here. A single thoughtless act could bring the pot to the boil right now.'

The Spaniard regarded him for longer than he should, before saying, harshly: 'Yes, sir.'

'Move out.'

The horsemen trampled mud and water and sloshed their way from the village, spare horses tailing. The tribesmen watched them go with eyes that burned like live coals in the dark openings of their huts.

The rain continued to drift down, soaking everything, water trickling down under the madder-red scarves and under the metal of the loricae, most miserably. The military cloaks gave some protection; but the men of the Ninth grumbled and mumbled about this accursed country where everything dissipated in rain and mist. The Spanish half turma rode into the camp and Marcus took himself off at once to Publius Popilius Pothinus. He handed over his messages and orders and then went off to find a fire and some food.

The camp looked like any other Roman marching camp. If the old foot-sloggers of the Legions had to march across Hades, that infernal place would be pock-marked by the marching camps thrown up each night. There was a formula by which the correct size of camp might be built to accommodate different strengths from three legions to a cohort. The surveyors with their instruments would select the spot and measure up the straight lines and the angles, and the legionaries would dig and throw up the ramparts and plant their stakes, and the leather tents would rise all in their ordered rows, the praetorium would loft grandly over all, and the Eagle and the standards would be given their place in the inner sanctum. The treasure chest would be buried, the clerks would have their offices, and life would proceed along well-oiled grooves.

Here the calculations had been made in the usual fashion. Each short side of the camp had to be a distance arrived at by taking the square root of the number of cohorts and multiplying by two hundred. The long sides would be one and a half times that figure. The corners would be rounded. Oh, yes, as Marcus steamed by a fire and gobbled hot porridge and drank tart vinegar, he was as aware of the ways of the legions as any man.

And, too, he was aware of the thrilling along his limbs, the tic in his eyelids, the twitch of his lips. He could barely stand still and force the porridge down. The vinegar tasted of ambrosia. Here, in this camp, were the two! Two!

Maecilius Severus.

Julius Priscus.

Two of the bastards. Marcus knew himself to be a vicious and intemperate young man. How he forced himself not to rush off and smash these two insolent whoresons into the ground he did not know. What he recognized was that he was growing older and more mature, a man who pondered vengeance before acting, a man who would not jeopardize the whole for the part. There was fat Crassus lolling in his villa in Pompeii. He would not be left out. There were two others besides these two here. Yes, the man who sought too eagerly for the eggs in the nest was like to slip from the tree.

The rain sifted down and the day warmed and the men grumbled, for the night would see a rapid and stealthy advance on a rebel strongpoint – one of the old oppida, those ancient hill-forts that had so signally failed the Britons before and yet to which they so readily resorted in moments of peril or defiance.

Just how many tribesmen there were out there no one seemed to know. Pothinus was not plentifully supplied with troops. Besides the cohort from the Ninth he had an auxiliary cohort and three turmae of cavalry auxilia – the half turma Marcus had brought making the total cavalry strength up to just over a hundred swords.

The men set about their preparations with the methodical routine of old hands, and as they formed up in the mizzle of rain and shook out into marching order, so Marcus formed his plans to take Maecilius Severus and Julius Priscus and deal with them as they deserved.

Just because the whoreson was a Julian wouldn't save him. Marcus had heard of this Priscus, a fat, overbearing, snobbish blot who would scarcely comprehend how he had sinned when Marcus told him. But – he'd find out, oh yes, by Mithras, he'd find out!

The offer Marcus had made to go and scout the camp of the Celts within the oppidum had been refused. He could not find any sorrow in him over that. Pothinus, a fat, sweaty and yet dedicated legionary who knew what was what, did say: 'If there is a check, Julius Britannicus, I shall request your assistance at that point. Meanwhile you would do well to attach yourself to the staff – such as it is.'

'Very good,' said Marcus. Young as he was, Marcus because of the system might rank as senior to this man; he was well content to let the centurionate take control, as they so often did when the crisis came.

As usual the centuries were under strength; the cohort from Legio VIIII mustered barely four hundred and the auxiliary cohort not many more. Less than a thousand men, to storm and take a massive earthwork, ringed by ditches and ramparts – yet this was the stuff on which the Roman armies cut their teeth.

Through the long falling lines of rain the long trudging lines of men slogged out.

The turf was a mere mud slick beneath his hands and knees. The rain beat into his face. The temperature was down enough to make him conscious of the exposed portions of skin, and curse, and slog upwards among the hundreds of men creeping like mud-slimed worms through the pitch darkness. Long before the moon rose the auxiliaries must be over the outer three ramparts and across their insanely-wide ditches and into the inner enclosures. The auxiliaries, hard-swearing men from Gaul, would do their work and the legionaries would arrive up to take over and finish. Between them the Romans would have the strength – just.

The sentries up there were most probably standing miserably cursing the rain and darkness, for all they were inured to the island weather. The Gauls snaked upwards, mud-slimed, furtive yet determined. Marcus, with the second wave ready to do whatever needed to be done from leading a charge to bringing up the legionaries, spat mud from a clogged mouth, cursed, and inched his way on. A man before him slipped and his sword rattled against his shield. Marcus could barely make the man out; before he could get up and take the man's name for tomorrow's punishment detail, the auxiliary scrambled on to vanish in the darkness. Well, that was as clear an indication as any of the old adage; the good legionary – and in this case the good auxiliary – should fear his centurion's vine stick more than the weapons of the enemy.

Abruptly the night split open. Shrieks and yells beat back down the slope. Marcus stood up and quite uselessly waved his sword. He yelled.

'On! On! Get up there! Into them!'

Everyone was clambering up over the middle wall, slipping and sliding down in mud to the bottom of the ditch and fighting up the farther face. Marcus scrabbled along, coated with mud, wet-through, feeling the blood piercing through him as his muscular exertions drove heat through his body. By Mithras! This was a far cry from the campaign against Masada!

The darkness remained intense, and that darkness was increased by the sputtering glow of torches flaming on the last wall. The Celts had run up from their watchfires, kept alight like those of the Romans by angled shelters against the rain, waving torches. Specks of light soared up to curve down on to the heads of the attackers. The Celts were trying to illuminate the Romans. Blazing bundles of dried grasses, spitting and sputtering as the rain drops hit them, arched high to fall and blaze for a few moments before they were quenched. In that pallid refractory light the slingers hurled. Panting up the last slope Marcus felt a heavy body collide with him, heard the man's grunt. He put out a hand and touched warm wet stickiness as the man's helmet fell off.

'On! On! Up!'

Now they were at the crest. A pack of chequered trousers and blankets before him, pale faces white smudges in the fireglow, arms whirling, the whine and hiss of slung pebbles. His gladius jumped forward, a man went down. Another took his place. The Celts were howling and dancing, and the Gauls were bellowing in reply. The moon would be up at any moment, its watery light quite enough to see to finish the job.

In a few moments of heady cut and thrust the Celts were thrown back. Their tribal pride would not allow any thought of retreat. On they came again, and the two masses of men locked, only to recoil as the Gauls, thrusting on, forced the Britons further back, down the reverse slope into the central hollow of the oppidum.

Then the legionaries arrived.

In a solid wave of iron the legionaries swamped over the last remaining flickers of resistance.

The whole affair had taken less than half an hour.

Pothinus was bellowing. A centurion was chasing up from the darkness, the moon now picking out the glitter of his harness. Marcus halted, flicking blood from his sword. On the trampled mud a Celt lay holding his intestines unbelievingly, dying in the mud and rain.

'A parcel of the bastards ran off!' shouted the centurion. He looked angry.

'They'll make south and west,' said Pothinus. The man was of the army, accustomed to thinking in army ways. 'We've not done the job properly here. They must be pursued, overtaken and destroyed.'

He rapped out his orders, what centuries to take up the pursuit, what to finish up here, what to return to camp to make sure of the base. Everyone scurried, everything was a whirl of action. Marcus was thoroughly accustomed to this iron-hard decision-making, of thinking on the feet. He snatched his horse's reins as a slave ran up, the cavalry were already trotting out. 'And remember,' Pothinus shouted. 'Every last one of the sons of bitches! All of them – to the sword!'

So it was horses again, the wiry hill ponies of Britain. They had recurred so often in this sojourn in Britain, and now they would be called on again to pursue the fleeing Celts in their chariots. Well, a Roman understood these things. A half-Roman half-Briton understood them twice as well.

Pothinus had committed all his cavalry in the chase. With them rode Marcus – and with them rode also Maecilius Severus and Julius Priscus.

Marcus saw the hand of Mithras in this work.

The hunting dogs would follow and if the rain eased on the morrow would be given the task of sniffing out every last one of the rebels. That work held no delights for Marcus. Head bent against the rain he rode. And ever and anon he looked with a look baleful and malignant at the two men he had sworn to kill.

The rain had stopped and the pursuit went relentlessly on. The weather had now turned and winter, which had so far shown his fangs in gales and rain and mists, now sharpened up his bitter attack with sleet and a ringing coldness and the grey threat of coming snow. It was now four days before the Ides of November. Just how many rebellious natives had been slain no one could say; the Romans took up whom they could and slew whom they must and the rest were sold into slavery.

That way someone reaped a little profit.

Down towards the south and west the pursuit continued; and now reports came in clearly telling of the collapse of this futile revolt. Once the Romans with their tiny force had smashed the locus of infection all the tribes had decided their truest destiny lay with Rome. Now every man's hand was turned against those foolish men who had sought to return to the old days before the Romans came.

'By Venus!' exclaimed Maecilius Severus, reining up his horse, hugging his cloak more tightly about him. The day was dry but cold, ears and noses were burning. Marcus turned away from the man, going to the far end of the line of marching men. No opportunity had so far presented itself. True to the iron resolve within him to deal with every one of his mother's murderers and not to commit the folly of being arrested and tried and condemned for simple justice, he had refrained – somehow – from degutting the two bastards on the spot.

Truly, he was a changed man from the impetuous youth of yesterday!

The dogs sniffed on eagerly. Chequered trousers had been thrust under their damp noses, they had sniffed; now they bayed deeply, a rolling menacing sound, and trotted along, heads low and tails high, like a forest of raised whips.

What those dogs would do to the fugitives when they caught them brought to mind some of the vivid descriptions in the plays of Seneca – not the great Lucius Annaeus of that name but the popular playwright – and of the fountains of blood, the loins pierced by branches, the bodies ripped apart by maddened animals, the bodies squashed and pulverized by the beaks of warships. The audiences of Rome these days had a love for the gloomy, the macabre, the hideous and the ghastly.

Now Maecilius Severus, pulling his horse around cruelly with the bronze bit gouging into the soft skin of his mouth, shouted violently as the dogs strained against their leashes.

'Let them go, you fools! They scent their quarry!'

Obediently, frightened, the slaves handling the hounds let them slip and, with shrill ululations, the animals bounded away.

With a wild hallooing the horsemen followed, leaving the foot-sloggers to keep up as best they could.

Marcus kicked his horse and turned his head to follow, keeping distances between himself and the hated figures of Severus and Priscus. Julius Priscus had made some attempt at conversation, seeing they were both Julians; but Marcus had cut him dead – and a fresh example of his uncouth manners was thereby known. Marcus cared little for that. They thundered along, the hooves ringing against the hard ground. The frost had been severe. Soon the snow would come and then life would be absolutely intolerable outside the thermae.

The hounds split into smaller parties followed by the riders and soon Marcus, who would not let either Priscus or Severus out of his sight, pounded along with them after a parcel of dogs who leaped, blazing with excitement, on the trail of quarry who ran and staggered and fell. They picked themselves up, shrieking, arms over their heads, running and stumbling again, only to fall once more as the dogs pounced upon them.

The sight meant nothing to Marcus, inflamed with passions he had struggled so resolutely to suppress.

Even the rending screams of a woman as she went down with the hounds tearing at her swollen belly, her face a blur of whiteness, her hair a cloud of driven shadow, could mean nothing beside the two men who must die. These scenes were familiar. The Roman Empire was builded upon slave labour. Slaves came and slaves went. Marcus felt the horse beneath him, felt the jar of his hooves against the iron-hard earth, felt the keen bite of the wind searing into his eyes and cheek, and he bore on, relentlessly following where Priscus and Severus led.

Salvius and Paulinus had paid. Now it was the turn of these two. Cold though the air struck, moisture came to Marcus's mouth, saliva tasting bitter and green, bilious with the promise of the gall to come.

All this country was heavily wooded with knolled elevations and rounded hills divided by steep and treacherous valleys. The whole pack poured down between flanking hills, recklessly helter-skeltering on after fugitives ahead. The Celts had some horses and the pursuit was not over yet. The hard ground rang with the noise of the hunt. Priscus and Severus parted, each following on a fork in the descending slope of the narrow valley. Marcus hesitated. It was not that he had a preference for one or the other, only that he felt some sign, some indication might be vouchsafed him in so serious a matter.

To the right Severus galloped on recklessly, the small group of cavalry with him roaring on after, the hounds ahead like avenging furies. To the left Priscus's horse skidded on the frosty ground. The man wrenched at the reins and compounded the mischief. His horse fell like a steer poleaxed in the shambles.

Horrified, Marcus lashed his own beast forward.

'Julius Priscus!' bellowed Marcus. 'You are unharmed! I pray all the gods you are not dead! I would not have you die for the pearls Cleopatra tossed to Mother Nile!'

Priscus scrambled up, shaking with anger. He kicked the horse, which neighed in agony, a leg stuck out at an unnatural angle. The pack of hounds vanished into the lower shadows and the two cavalrymen who turned back saw Marcus.

'Go on!' bellowed Marcus in his best parade-ground manner. 'Fools! Do not let a man get away — those were your orders! Don't stand gaping like dolts! Ride!'

'Yes, sir!' they shouted and wheeled their horses and galloped away. The air steamed with the breaths of horses and men alike. The leafless branches of trees stretched over the descending trail like skeletal arms offering shelter to corpses.

'Stupid whoreson nag! Feet like grease-boards! I'm winded—' Priscus glanced up, one hand holding his back, the other rubbing a shoulder. He glared at Marcus. 'And what has made you so suddenly concerned over my skin, Britannicus? I do not owe you money. I have not borrowed your parade helmet — so?'

'This place is damned cold,' said Marcus. 'There is a cave above the river bank.' As he spoke the first snow flakes fell, silently, ghostlike, gossamer drifting whitenesses so fragile so gentle, and the forerunners of an army mightier than any Rome might boast.

Priscus caught a flake on his palm. He looked at it and then as the cold bit wiped it away on his cloak. He shuddered.

'Let us go to this god-forsaken cave, then,' he said. He shouldered off, lifting his cloak to shield his face from the gently drifting snow.

'Your horse,' said Marcus. 'The beast has a broken leg. You will not walk off and leave him?'

'The beast is useless. He should not have fallen — if you want to slit his throat — that is your affair.'

There was no room in Marcus's heart for further rage against this man. Coldly, he whipped out his pugio and, kneeling on the horse's head and ignoring the animal's snorts and screams, he drew the blade across the corded throat. Dark blood gushed. The blood smoked into the damp grass and melting snowflakes glistened upon the widening pool.

Marcus stood up as the horse convulsed and heaved and so

died. He walked down the twisting path to the cave entrance with a determined tread.

Priscus parted the depending brambles, looking into the darkness distastefully.

'I suppose we had best shelter here until they return for us. Unless—' He half-turned, looking back over his shoulder where the heavy cloak lay in folds already glistening with melted snow.

'Unless?'

'Unless I take your horse and send help for you.' Priscus brightened. 'Yes, that would be best.'

'There is something I wish to tell you, first. Go into the cave out of the snow, Priscus.'

Somehow, Marcus's words were uttered in a normal voice; for all that Priscus glanced at him sharply before going into the cave entrance.

As he followed Marcus looked up. Against the solid wall of blackness ahead a spark glowed. A light! Here in the bowels of the earth!

Instantly, he recognized what the light must mean.

Priscus understood, also. He drew his gladius, silently, and the hunched shape of him took on power and bulkiness. For the moment Marcus was content to find out what the light really meant, and if, indeed, it meant what he suspected, to deal with that first. Both men advanced into the cave with naked steel in their hands. Julius Britannicus wanted no witnesses to what he intended here.

The entrance arched, a series of slab-like rock formations frowning over the portal. Inside the cave resembled a corridor, rough and irregular in form, misted with the beads of water seepage, slippery underfoot, and musty with the dank smell of ages. Creeping on, the two Romans felt the warmth of the place, warmer than the frigid outside air. A few paces from the fire they halted.

Two men and a woman huddled around the tiny blaze, their chequered blankets eloquent of their race.

Priscus stiffened. The fire gave enough light to make out details. At the side of the two men lay shields, spears and the long Celtic swords. Priscus, chafing at delay, incensed by his fall, savage in his humour, was in no mind to give the Britons half a chance.

Without a shout, with a lethal rush, Priscus charged.

Before the men could turn or leap up the deadly gladius did its work. Both men screeched and doubled over, feeling the blood leaking from their riven sides. A Roman knew the place to stick a sword.

'Move a muscle, girl, and you are dead also,' shouted Priscus. He snaked the sword at her, so the dark drops could fly to spatter her dress.

'So you Romans have found us out, even here,' she said. 'Very well, Roman butcher. I do not fear you. Strike me down now with the blood of my brothers on your weapon!'

Her accent was very good for a native. Marcus listened.

Priscus laughed. He found great humour in the situation.

'I think not, slut. I think I shall teach you Roman manners before we send you off to the slave block.'

There was only one meaning behind his words.

The girl clutched an object at the end of a string about her neck. She looked pinched and worn; but Marcus did not fail to observe the beauty there, the face that in ordinary times would have been merry and lively, with the blue eyes and dark hair of this race, their laughter in the curves of her lips.

'The Master will preserve me, whatever you may do,' she said, and Marcus sighed at her words. The damned Stoic philosophy must have penetrated even here, to distant Britain. The Stoics meant well; but they would deny the gods and make mock of the Emperor. Their dream of a world-wide brotherhood of men was just that, a dream.

'Whatever I may do,' said Priscus. He laughed again. 'I shall do a great deal, slut, and you will obey me, or else—'

'I think, Julius Priscus,' said Marcus. 'That the time has come for me to tell you what it is needful for you to know.'

The fire in Marcus would not be damped down any longer. The gladius in his fist pointed at Priscus, a slender thread of reflection from the fire limning the blade.

The space in which the fire had been built opened out from the entrance corridor; vast stalactites and stalagmites held out yearning arms for one another, and others had melded so that veined and curiously sinuous and plastic forms filled the shadowed spaces. The whole place dripped with the moisture of the years.

'What in Hades are you prattling about, Britannicus? The wench is right for the ploughing – you may wait your turn—'

'You did this before, Priscus? Do you remember? When the

Ninth defeated the Brigantes? Six of you – and Crassus, let us not forget Crassus – six of you and the princess of the Iceni.'

Priscus stared. The fire cast a glow upon his face, and turned his eyes into hollow smudges, his mouth into a rounded O. 'You – what are you talking about?'

'Do you remember the night, Priscus? When you ravished the princess of the Iceni?'

'Of course I do! And I know you were a bratling from the barbarians, also. Your father – he was a simple-minded fool – and you are a whoreson-dog, Britannicus, to talk thus—'

'You knew the lady was a chieftainess of the Iceni, now in alliance with Rome. Yet you raped and murdered her.'

'She was a traitor! She had brought a great treasure to the Brigantes—'

'Ah! The treasure. Tell me of the treasure, Priscus.'

'The devil I will! You'd best watch your tongue, Britannicus. Better still, go back to the cave entrance and see if they have returned for us yet. I have a ploughing with this wench—'

'You'll rape no more girls – or grown women with sons, you bastard!'

'Sons—'

Priscus saw it all. And even as he saw so his bloodied blade switched up and he drove mercilessly at Marcus.

With a laugh – a laugh that sounded like the frenzied cry of a demon in torment – Marcus swirled his own sword up, took the gladius upon it, swung, twisted, sent Priscus's sword high into the air to clang against the rocks and clatter into silence.

'You whoreson dog! You heap of dung! Yes, Priscus – yes! *My mother!* And now you are going to suffer, suffer as you've never believed a man could suffer!'

'Keep off!' Priscus yelled and sprang back. He glared about, looking this way and that, into the shadows, like a rat trapped by hounds, seeking a way of escape. And all the time the girl crouched by the fire, silent, her hands gripping the object that swung from her neck, and her eyes darting from one Roman to the other.

'You're going to suffer, Priscus!' The gladius snicked out with such speed that Priscus was caught unaware. His left ear fell, followed by a splashing flow of blood. 'Bit by bit, Priscus you will be carved – for I will not soil my hands on you as I did the others.'

At this Priscus yelled. His eyes glared white and fey through the darkness, the firelight spurting at that moment and throwing writhing ghastly shadows about the ancient chamber.

'The others! Paulinus! Salvius! It was you! I heard and shrugged—' The pain from his ear dulled and to remind him and keep him up to the work Marcus feinted at his guts, switched the blade up and sliced off the other ear.

Priscus shrieked. He spun about, like a drunken man at Saturnalia, stumbled a few paces away. The girl sat up. Priscus still shrieking blundered blindly into a wall where a fall of rocks, jagged edged and clean, told of a recent collapse.

The girl said, very quickly: 'Have a care, Roman. The roof is treacherous—'

'Help! Help!' Priscus shouted, crabbing along the wall, feeling with his hands like butterflies before him. Marcus followed, the firelight bouncing from the bloodied blade, moving after him with remorselessness that drove anguish and utter horror into the heart of Priscus.

How he'd cut the bastard up! He'd slice his hide into little pieces! This was the whoreson bastard who had raped and tortured his mother. No idea other than to make Priscus's death as painful as possible could enter Marcus's heart now.

A voice shouted, high, booming in the cavern. A voice from another world.

'Ho! Priscus! Where are you! Is Britannicus there, also?'

Maecilius Severus! Come back from the hunt, come back to find his comrade!

Priscus started up from the wall, his face blazing with renewed hope. He lifted up his head.

'Maecilius Severus! I am here – and Britannicus is a madman! He knows – he knows of the Iceni bitch and her treasure!' Priscus gasped out the words, gabbling, shrieking, his face grotesque in the half-light. 'She was his mother, Severus! *His mother!*'

SEVEN

The words rang and reverberated in the cavern. Marcus cursed. This place sawed at a man's nerves. He had thought to accomplish a part of his just vengeance, and now it seemed he was fatally betrayed. The girl started up, agitated.

On the right of the cave the dark gleam of sliding water showed where the river ran through. The firelight speckled back, white and glistening from the pendant arrays of stalactites in a great curtain. Beyond, the feeling of a vaster space lay shrouded in eternal blackness.

Priscus did not shout again. He saw that there was no way past Marcus to the cave entrance. As Marcus started for him he gulped and ran. The girl shouted.

Priscus ran full into the wall of rock. He let fly a sob or a curse, intermingled with the grind of moving stone.

The girl caught at Marcus's left arm, pulling him back.

From the entrance Severus shouted.

'What's going on? Priscus! What is this about Britannicus?' The words boomed and echoed and rolled.

And then, above the shouts, above the grind of moving rock, a tremendous din of clashing cymbals broke through the caverns, setting the rock trembling, shaking the air, making the fire spurt and spark. An enormous cacophony of clashing cymbals, as though the last trump was being blown through all the secret spaces of the Earth.

'Demons!' shouted Marcus. The girl pulled him back.

He broke free, jumped forward to stick Priscus. The harsh grind of rock, sharp and sinister, warned him. Something moved above his line of vision. He stooped, snatched a burning brand from the fire, held it aloft.

In the smoky blaze he saw Priscus, backed flat against the wall, hands outspread. Above the man's head the world seemed to be moving. A slab, a gigantic slab of the rock, bowed out.

'Priscus!' shouted Marcus, and like a weird echo so Severus's shout bounced up: 'Priscus!'

The girl pulled hard at his upper arm, making the torch

waver and fleer distorted shadows. He tried to shake her off but she would not release him.

'Back, Roman! Or you share the fate of that monster!'

The rock moved and bowed and in the refractory light Marcus saw the block tilting. He jumped back with the girl. The block tilted, tilted, screeching like the rout of Cybele. It blotted out all sense and all reason and it fell, smoking dust and shards of rock into their eyes, shattering their ears with the din.

'By Mithras!' gasped Marcus, choking, feeling the rock chips jagging into him. He reeled back as the world before him blossomed into an ochre boil with the fire reflections swirling distorted from the bubble of dust. He stumbled back dragging the girl. The torch threw sheening reflections from the moisture-running walls.

And – he had seen!

He had seen, in the instant before that crushing weight bore down with so awful a power. He had seen Julius Priscus, flattened into a hollow in the rock, shrieking with fear, the terror making his eyes bulge and his jaw lock in an insane rictus of frenzy and horror and despair.

Oh, yes, Marcus Julius Britannicus would remember that frightful picture! He had not ripped the bastard limb from limb; the mysterious forces of the elemental worlds not to be understood by mere mortals had taken and destroyed the man. If Priscus had not been crushed beneath the block – and Marcus hoped he had not! For then the whoreson dog would be trapped. He would be trapped in total darkness in a living tomb!

That seemed a fitting end for one with his crimes.

'Priscus!' The voice battered at his senses. He started. It was as though a voice called to him from beyond the grave.

Then he saw the bulky form of Severus blunder into the radiance from the fire. The man had his sword out and his jaw was set and he looked murderous.

He stared at the two bodies of the Britons, and kicked them both to make sure they were dead.

The girl cried out, softly, at this.

'Severus!' cried Marcus.

'The noise—' Severus remained on guard. 'Priscus – where is Priscus?'

As Marcus did not answer but came on, the torch held high

and dragging the girl, his gladius stuffed away into the scabbard and fouling the lining with blood, Severus took a pace back.

'Come no closer, Britannicus! Where is Priscus? I heard what he said – so the slut was your dam, eh? Then right merrily we rode her! Aye, you mewling half-caste guttersnipe! Come a step closer and I'll cut you down out of hand!'

'Priscus is dead, you dog – or, if not dead then walled in a living tomb and dying from fear. And, Severus, raper of good women, you will die now, in your turn, screaming your guts out.'

With full and evil intent Marcus ran at the fellow, letting go of the girl and ripping out the gladius. The sword stuck, clogged with blood. Severus danced back, instantly alert, trying to keep his footing on the lime-watered stones, peering past the shadows to see Marcus more clearly by the light of the torch he carried. With a curse Marcus hurled the blazing brand full in Severus's face.

But the fellow was an old hand and not to be caught like that, with a simpleton's trick.

He batted the torch away with his sword and bore down, ready to cut or thrust as his opponent gave him opportunity.

Filled with the holy wrath that drove him on Marcus lunged and feinted and tried to cut Severus's arm. The gladii clashed and ground together and parted, and Severus leaped lightly back, laughing, shouting: 'Fool! You are no match for a swordsman! Prepare to die!'

With that he leaped in, cunning and quick and skilled, his sword a blur in the confusing half-darkness, with the fire and the fallen torch throwing conflicting shadows. Strong he was, this big bulky man, strong and quick and lithe. Marcus felt his foot slip on the edge of one of the huge slabs of rock, slip on the coating of rimed-water. He recovered and Severus's blade rasped his thigh below the pteruges, parting the leather and brass and gashing the flesh. The cut was not deep. But it annoyed Marcus. He could feel the blood trickling down his leg.

He shouted, suddenly, deliberately high so that the echoes rolled and rang in mock imitation of that supernal noise of clashing cymbals that had thundered up from the dark and secret recesses of the cave. He hurled forward and he cut down with a sure direction of blow. At that instant Severus stumbled over the corpse of one of the Britons. Marcus's blow flashed harmlessly past his arm.

Flat on the rock, Severus lay, one side bathed in the orange light of the fire, the other in the weaker radiance of the sputtering torch.

Marcus laughed. He wouldn't kill the bastard so quickly . . .

He leaned above Severus and with his left hand he whipped the Briton's chequered blanket across, enfolded the sword, jerked savagely, and so tore the weapon from Severus's hand. He threw the blanket down over Severus, bending down with the gladius at his throat.

'You will suffer before you die, bastard dog!'

The blanket-enwrapped man writhed, trying to squirm away and to fight free of the muffling folds of chequered cloth. His arms waved frenziedly over his body in a succession of wild passes designed to beat aside the blade he anticipated would strike slicing for his guts.

Marcus laughed. This was the way of it! He leaned down and he slashed Severus's right ear off. The blood splashed on to the blanket, as Severus screamed. This was the just vengeance! This would pay – just a little – for the horror his mother had endured.

He reached to slash the other ear away and the girl caught his arm, and pulled him. His foot slid on the slippery stone. He stumbled back, yelling with a fury at once insane and icy cold with intent.

'Think what you do, Roman!'

Sheer outrage struggled with the madness all scarlet within him. A Celtish bitch, trying to interfere with his destiny!

He would not strike her. He pushed her; but she clung like a thistle burr, crying that he imperilled all he hoped for of salvation. Severus scrabbled like a giant toad, the blanket all bloodied caught about him. Marcus saw the man he had sworn to kill, he saw the sheen of fire-light on the fantastic walls, the overarching veins lost in shadow.

'My salvation rests on the hope of Mithras! He abhors curs like these!'

And Marcus lunged forward, slashing as Severus blundered to his feet. A corner of the blanket cut free and fell. Marcus slashed again and the girl gripped his arm and Severus, screaming, vanished into the shadows past a corner of rock.

'Let go, girl, or I will cut you down!'

'My life means nothing! My brothers are dead! My people slain! But you – you I may yet save!'

Marcus could not understand her. He tried to shake her off and she hung on, like a small child at play.

'There is time for you to see the way!' she gasped out. 'Let me help you.'

Some dim understanding that the girl sincerely meant what she said penetrated through to Marcus. A twinge shook him, there through the scarlet blaze of destruction roaring in his brain. He ran and the girl ran with him, clinging. He snatched up the burning brand and held it aloft, the girl still dragging down his sword-arm, and so they ran to the cavern entrance.

Past sentinel rocks at the cavern entrance Marcus could see a white glimmer of falling snow. The cave opened on to the side of the hill. The sheer rock face was already clustered with snow and, abruptly, Marcus shivered.

They staggered from that awful spot, and as they felt the snow falling upon them, the last roaring clashing reverberated behind them, the thunder as of a thousand waterfalls smashing and crashing about them.

Maecilius Severus was just mounting up. He saw Marcus and the girl appear, like demons from the underworld, and he yelled and lashed his horse.

'Madman!' screamed Severus. 'I know! Now I know what Vellius Condorus meant! But you will never see the treasure and you will never slay me!'

There it was again, that name, Vellius Condorus.

A distant ululation began, growing nearer and wilder, and yet shot through with dismal howls. Marcus stared about for his horse; the beast was nowhere to be seen. The girl pulled his arm.

He shook her away; Severus wheeled the horse, a grey blur through the falling snow; the distant dogs howled again, mournfully. Where was his damned horse? Severus put his head down and lashed his horse and in only a few paces was lost in the swirling snowflakes. The cold bit in cruelly.

The whining of the hounds, the blood dropping down . . .

He swung back so violently the girl almost fell and, without thought, he caught her around the waist. He was cold now with purpose, a fresh resolve, a cold halo to the raging fires of vengeance he must use and control and never allow to overwhelm him in the madness that would destroy all.

He felt the girl's waist, lissom, smooth.

'This is an ancient place,' she said, not breaking away, holding him, no doubt believing in a victory. 'We Celts call it Wocov.' In the Celtish way she did not pronounce the double-you in the Wo sound. 'We have lived here for many years, and men and women lived here long before us – bones, skulls, stones, – and the witch, too—'

Marcus released her and pushed past, going back into the entrance. The corridor with its roughly natural series of steps glittered in the light of the fire, dying now, more ruby and orange than the bright blaze that had first greeted him. The girl pattered after, shivering. Marcus hunted along the damp stones.

The girl chattered on, a background, inconsequential, yet somehow inextricably mingled with the momentous events here. He would always remember her and the feel of her waist when he thought of Priscus, shrieking, insane with fear, penned beneath the smoking avalanche of rock.

'You Romans came here,' she said, following him. 'You put up a leaden tablet commemorating your pagan emperor Claudius.' Marcus darted forward, stooping. She said: 'But I do not think you are a Roman like the others.'

He bent, picked up the shorn scrap of bloodied cloth. With the trophy in his hand he looked again, further on, nearer the fire. The girl would not leave him; yet the bodies of her two brothers lay there, stark in death.

'What is your name, wench?'

'I am called Gwenhwyvar. But I have been given the name of Mary—'

'Mary – a strange name to find in Britain.'

'There is much you do not understand, Roman – I heard you called Britannicus. That must explain—'

'Yes, yes, and here is that damned fellow's ear!' And, with an exulting grab, Marcus snatched up Severus's severed ear.

'I see, Britannicus, I see you seek your vengeance and I can understand why. But I tell you that vengeance is no man's. Vengeance is the Lord's—'

'Aye! And Mithras will strengthen my hand!'

He ran back to the entrance, slipping and sliding, mounting the slope of irregular steps. This place choked into the guts of a man, this Wocov, despite its warmth against the icy air outside. The torch threw a streaming hair of light upon this girl, this

Gwenhwyvar who was called Mary. Why she should be called that name here, in Britain, Marcus had no idea. He felt the pull of her, her lissomness. She was beautiful, intense, concerned over him. Her deep bosom moved with her concern beneath the thin dress and he could see where the ripped-away fibula had torn the material to reveal a glimpse of white skin.

'Will nothing prevent you seeking out this man who committed this horrible crime – and slaying him?'

'This is no concern of yours, Mary. By Mithras! I will seek them all out! My lares – do you think my ancestors would let me rest, would they not mock me through all the years, if I failed? And yet, why do I waste time talking to you . . .' He moved out into the snow. The white stuff had fallen thickly enough to lay. The sky was freighted with more snow to come. The whole world drizzled a grey choking blanket of white and black, suffocating, clenching, driving thoughts and feelings inward.

'And me?' demanded Mary who had been Gwenhwyvar. 'Am I not a Briton, a rebel, one to be made slave?'

'As for you, girl, hide yourself away until we are all gone. And may Mithras whom I serve join with Venus to preserve you.'

The dogs were panting and snuffling up the trail, coming up to the cave entrance. Marcus's horse, disturbed, walked before them, head hanging, the reins drawing lines through the snow. In this apparition, Marcus saw afresh the hand of Mithras. He laughed, joyously, knowing that right and justice rode with him. He threw the torch to the girl, this Mary who had been Gwenhwyvar, and she caught it dexterously.

'May the light of the Saviour shine on you, Roman, Britannicus!'

He grasped the horse and mounted up with a swing. She was a brave wench – and she had the courage to call upon Mithras, upon the Saviour, to aid him! These Stoics, as all the world knew, were deeply contemptuous of gods. Vespasian for all his clemency had had to deal harshly with them.

Mithras was the god of the Legions. To hear his name in the mouth of a Celtic girl, a Briton born to be a slave, sounded odd. He lashed the horse along towards the dogs.

'Look out for yourself, girl! If the dogs scent you . . .'

'I must go back and mourn my dead. Even though my brothers have gone into the radiance of the Light, still shall I weep.'

But Marcus was galloping away and hallooing to the dogs and shaking out the pieces of bloodied blanket and the severed ear . . .

For the last three miles the snow had ceased falling and the trail of the horseman ahead stretched in sooty splotches against the whiteness. Greyness everywhere betokened another heavy fall; but for now the air glimmered with a strange white light through the greyness, turning trees and shrubs into ghostly icicles, making objects distorted and gigantic. The dogs moved with less fervour than before, cold and hungry as they must be. But Marcus shouted and cursed, lashing them on with his whip. Somewhere ahead a man rode a faltering horse through the snow, and Marcus had to come up with him and slay him before he found a friendly Roman encampment in this desolation of snow.

They had ridden to the north and had come a fair six miles.

Marcus sat erect and peered ahead. The trees hung with dripping whiteness obscured all vision and the few open rides only led on to fresh groves of the ghostly trees.

Suddenly, as though the statue of Janus had been turned, one of the leading hounds belled a deep baying note.

Others took it up. A howling mingled chorus broke from the dogs. They moved faster, their bodies seeming to become leaner and longer, and they trotted over the snow, splashing here and there through deeper drifts. They knew their quarry blundered along ahead of them, and they knew, too, that the sooner they caught and despatched the victim the quicker they would be released from this icy bondage and allowed to return to their quarters. Marcus peered ahead, trying to see, aware of the undulations of the ground beneath the snow, seeing the trees thinning, seeing a misty stretch of land opening up with a configuration he could not at first determine.

The rider ahead of him had pulled up and was now angling along to the right.

'Severus,' said Marcus, to himself, his fist clenching on his whip. 'That can only be Severus – and I've got the bastard now.'

The dogs scrabbled forward eagerly, the scent of finality giving them the strength to run with some of their old fierce impetuousness. Marcus kicked his horse's flanks and the tired beast responded. This was the last throw.

The fugitive saw them. He looked back and he flung up an arm. Then his horse bounded forward.

'After him! After him!' roared Marcus. 'Pull him down!'

The dogs bayed and rushed, the snow flying from their paws, their tails high, their tongues lolling.

The man ahead drove his horse hard and the beast, maddened by continual blows from the whip, galloped blindly. The rider swung to his left and Marcus saw him put his head down and smash on, sheets of snow fountaining away from the flying hooves.

Over the uproar of baying hounds, of the snorts of the horses, the slushing suck of the snow, Marcus yelled. He filled his lungs and roared out in a high ringing voice.

'Maecilius Severus! You cannot escape my just wrath! You will die for your crimes—'

The rider ahead vanished.

Marcus cursed, thinking the man was eluding him down some unsuspected valley. He drove his horse on and the dogs were pulling up, circling, sniffing, the snow smothering them, wildly excited, as though a wolf had eluded them by some devilish wolfish trick.

The horse plunged among the hounds who yelped and backed away.

'Mithras! The mouth of hell!'

Marcus hauled his shivering horse up. He lay back on the reins pulling with all his strength. The horse screamed, a high-pitched whinny of utter fear. Amid a scurry of snow and a convulsive leg-kicking fury the horse somehow kept his balance. He halted, shivering, blowing huge clouds of steam, frightened witless.

Slowly, Marcus dismounted into the snow. His feet crunched unpleasantly into the white crust, and he felt coldness strike through the thick woollen and leather linings to his military boots. Cautiously, he approached the lip of the precipice.

'Now Mithras held me safe!' he said, in awe. He looked down, feeling the giddiness upon him.

From far below came the thudding, squashing sound of Severus and his horse striking the rocks, the long-drawn-out scream dwindling away to a series of attenuating echoes, most dolefully.

The gorge slashed through the countryside. It turned and twisted, its side sheer rock falls. Far, far below, the bottom lay like the vision of a madman caught in delirium. The size and the grandeur of the gorge filled Marcus with a divine inspiration of will, as though Mithras and all his ancestors had driven the rapist-murderer Severus expressly to this spot. The man had been crazed with fear with his nemesis and the pack of slavering hounds on his trail and ridden his horse blindly over the edge, spinning out and falling to pulverize his bones on the rocks beneath, to splash his blood and scatter his brains upon the snow-covered ground.

'And damnation to you, you bastard, Severus!'

Thus was the epitaph spoken over the grave of Maecilius Severus.

EIGHT

Metellus Curtius.

Suetonius Postumus.

These two remained – not forgetting, of course, fat Crassus away there in Pompeii. And there was this sub-procurator he was now to see, this Vellius Condorus. His name had been mentioned by men who had done those unspeakable things to his mother, the name Condorus uttered as though the man had something to do with the crime.

The fire of just vengeance in Marcus burned as fiercely and as purely bright as before. There could be no rest until justice had been done, a justice he could never receive under Roman law and therefore a justice he had been forced to take into his own hands. But he had not been forced. He took a great and holy joy in ridding the world of these sinful men.

The snow lay thickly everywhere and men's breaths plumed frost from their raw throats. Everybody coughed and sneezed, and inflamed eyes and funerealy dripping noses marked the course of the Romans through the land of mist.

Marcus felt little discomfort, his years away from the island of his birth had done little to reduce his vigour and health. He strode through the wooden halls with an upright carriage, alert, his left hand resting on the hilt of his sword. As an officer he carried the gladius slung on the left. He could not carry the vine stick, that ancient emblem of the centurionate; but everything about him marked him as a man high in the favour of the governor, a man to be watched, a man whose favour in its turn should be curried.

The prisoners squatted outside in the snow, disconsolate, scraps of cloth over their heads, and they keened a doleful threnody of pain as they waited for their fates to be decreed.

The auxiliary on guard over them banged his feet about to get the warmth back; but he was a Gaul and somewhat accustomed to snow and cold. Marcus saw him stiffen up as the equerry approached.

Marcus was in a hurry. He wanted to get back to Frontinus

and see about the most important thing in his life, see about the lives of Curtius and Suetonius Postumus.

He saw the girl.

She huddled against the wall, small and shrivelled, the snow dusting her dark hair and shoulders, the old blanket tattered and threadbare about her little protection against the cold. Marcus saw her and walked on and without a pause passed her by. If she saw him she gave no sign.

The sub-procurator was a man of middle years, making his way up in the Roman world, a man of Equestrian rank, intolerant of those set under his authority, a man toadying to those above him. He eyed Marcus. Marcus knew enough of the specialized world of the procurators to know they loved their work, they loved the heavy feel of gold through their fingers, they could spend hours adding up their figures and calculating their sums. The rapaciousness of the treasury officials had been one vital factor in the insurrection led by his great aunt Boudicca.

'Well met, Julius Britannicus,' said this Vellius Condorus, a hearty geniality masking his thoughts. A heavy, prematurely-bald man, with red-rimmed eyes and heavy jowls, the thick neck of the Roman giving dignity to a coarse face. 'You must be cold – I will have warmed wine brought, mulsum – the British make the finest honey – come, stand here where the floor is warmer nearer the flue . . .'

He wore the decent white and he acted the busy host. Marcus made the necessary replies, a little coldly; Condorus affected not to notice. Their work could be glossed over in a quarter of a clepsydra's cycle. Yes, the Dumnonii had been stupid and refractory, burning corn wagons, smashing oil amphorae. The tax demands had been heavy; but the Empire demanded, and what would you?

Marcus knew, as all the world knew, that what the Empire demanded was added to, and added to most heavily, by those who collected the taxes.

The wine sweetened with honey was brought, the mulsum being the traditional opening round in the drinking at a feast; clearly this Condorus liked it for its own sake; the swelling at his waist told its own story. As he drank Marcus noted down all the details he must report back to the governor.

Then: 'I see you have prisoners, Vellius Condorus. I am in

114

need of a slave – a woman to wash and mend and do what is necessary—'

'Of course, my dear Britannicus! Nothing simpler. I will have one brought to you – you are putting up here, of course?'

'No. I must push on immediately. The governor is waiting to hear what has been accomplished here.' Marcus considered, and added: 'The Legions are fully committed. He will recall the vexillation of the Ninth, and the auxilia. A few turmae will suffice here, I think, now.'

'Yes, yes, of course.'

These Equestrians! How they hustled to agree with every word uttered by a patrician! Even if that patrician was a half-caste, a man with a noble Roman father and some pagan painted savage for a mother . . .

The conversation might have wended on; but Marcus was in no mood for polite commonplaces. He bustled. The girl was selected. She lifted her head and snow slid from the blanket and the fall of hair, and she looked at him once, then she lowered her eyelids in exhaustion. She did not say a word. A fresh horse was brought out and saddled up and Marcus paid for the girl and for an ass for her to ride. Condorus made further attempts to persuade him to stay; Marcus would not budge. With his half turma of Spanish cavalry about him he rode out into the hostile whiteness of this island, this land of mist that was his birthplace.

It began to snow again.

No rational Roman would travel in snow.

Marcus was forced to quarter his men in the miserable sod and thatch huts of the next village, turfing out the occupants, complaining but obeying, and there he had to spend the night fretting at the delay.

The Spanish decurion came in to report an odd occurrence.

A small party of horsemen had been observed following. The cavalryman, true to his instincts, had sent a couple of his men to reconnoitre on which the other horsemen had wheeled their mounts and vanished into the driving swirls of snow.

'Were they Britons?'

'They looked like these damned Dumnonii, sir. But there was something about 'em – the way they rode – stiffly – if it wasn't a thing Bacchus would crow over I'd say they looked like Romans astride horses too small for 'em.'

'Thank you, decurion,' said Marcus. 'If they bother us tomorrow you have my permission to do what is necessary.' He did not miss the instinctive movement of the cavalryman's hand to his sword hilt. 'And for tonight make sure the guard stays awake. I'll make the rounds later. You probably have no need to remind your men what happens to a man who sleeps on guard duty . . .'

'No, sir. They've all seen – not a pretty sight for a squeamish stomach; but mighty convincing—'

'That will be all.'

'Sir!'

The decurion left the small house, a mere hut, in which Marcus had quartered himself and his new slave girl.

The earth had been dug out into a depression leaving a platform at one side serving as a bed. In the centre a fire crackled, the wood ruthlessly obtained by the Spaniards for the military aide, as they had taken the wood for their own fire. The smoke wafted around before drifting through the hole in the thatched roof. Bugs of all kinds droned and twittered and bit and stung, hiding inside away from the winter.

The girl lay on the bed, shivering.

Marcus warmed his hands at the fire. The food had been plentiful and of good quality, as Condorus had insisted they take ample provisions. Now Marcus stared at the girl.

'You are cold?'

'A little.' She stared back. Her eyes caught the firelight and gleamed. She lay back under the chequered blanket, and her feet in their crude leather and stuffed-rag sandals protruded. The feet were filthy, and blue with cold.

'Why did you buy me – master?'

The last word would have by its inflexion and intonation have provoked an instant whipping in any well-run Roman household.

Marcus took up the goblet of wine from the floor. It had been warmed and was now rapidly cooling. Even their breaths steamed in the hut despite the fire. He drank it all off and threw the goblet into a corner, then poked the fire and piled more wood, carefully. The smoke stung the eyes.

'I do not know, Gwenhwyvar.'

Some feeling of pity for her, a sudden spurt of compassion,

not understood, not even wanted? Something like that. He moved to the bed. She lay back, not so much like a cowed kitten as a wary cat, drawing back ready to arch her back and spring.

'I am your slave. But slavery is a merely mortal state.'

He knew what she was suggesting.

'You Stoics always amaze me. You would pull all Rome down if you could. And yet, often, you speak as though you follow Mithras—'

'Mithras!'

She laughed; but the sound was weak and followed by coughing.

Marcus threw down his military cloak, threw it down over her body. He bent to tuck the sides in. Her eyes slid over him, her lashes very black and long and curling.

'Why do you treat a mere slave like—'

'I have told you, girl. I do not know. I should whip you.'

'You may do so, if that is your wish.'

'By the Names! Your insolence would drive Jupiter himself to laughter.'

'Jupiter! You and these false idols. There is only one Saviour, one Light—'

'Aye! There is! The cult of Emperor one must follow if one is prudent in these days. One does not prate of Mithras to any stranger. But you – a Stoic – I do not understand.'

'No, my master. You do not understand.'

'And it is damned cold here and we may keep ourselves warm together.'

Her eyes closed as he climbed on to the straw of the bed and snuggled down under the blankets and cloaks. He was aware of her body beside him, could feel the warmth. He moved closer. Presently he put out a hand and touched her body. She did not move. He said: 'Why do you say nothing, Gwenhwyvar?'

'My fate is already decided. Here on this earth I have a mere body, of clay, filled with sin. When the Saviour wills it I shall join him in Everlasting Glory—'

'That is so.'

He moved again, and cupped her breast. She was firm and hard, yet soft and supple. Her breast stood up hard under his hand yet she lay flat on her back. He stroked down her stomach, under the blanket, pulling her dress away, feeling the silkiness of her skin, the curly hair, the warmth and sweetness of her and she made no sign, no movement.

Presently, when he lay on top, she said: 'Is this what those men did to your mother – master?'

He stilled his movements. He was puzzled. 'No. No, I do not think so.' He thought. 'No. For they raped her. There were six of them – and fat Crassus – and they held her. If you had made a sign—'

'Are you saying if I cried out you would take your weapon away and leave me be. You already know I am a virgin.'

Marcus let his laugh sigh very gently through his lips.

'I do not think a team of elephants could stop me now, for I—'

'Yes, master. You are.'

'There is no sin in this.'

'Because I am your slave?'

'Why – no! And yet – why not because of that?'

'I believe that a woman has a right to her own body. And yet I am cold and tired and I cannot fight further. My brothers are dead, my mother and father long gone – and with the glorious life everlasting for them, in which I glory! Do what you will, Roman.'

Marcus leaned down and kissed her. She did not respond, her lips warm and soft. He kissed her again. He had some skill in kissing a girl. He remembered – vaguely – the way Rachel had kissed him, there below Masada. This girl, this Briton, this slave girl, she was sweet – sweet like a rich brown nut of Autumn, filled with ripe goodness, Presently he felt her arms go around his neck, and she kissed him back. Their bodies pressed closer. She began to gasp. Her breathing quickened, quickened into a rich hoarseness, a panting, a sudden wild and uncontrollable heaving. Marcus felt all the supernal fires of Etna bursting like molten lava, and he could do nothing else in all this world but hold her and let the spasms shake him.

When they lay quietly, she said: 'I am ashamed.'

'Because you enjoyed yourself?'

'I had thought the first time would be painful—'

'You are healthy, and have worked hard.'

She was stroking his hair. 'And you were gentle.'

'I seek those who were not gentle with my mother.'

'Forgiveness, master. That is what the Saviour tells us.'

'Forgiveness? For one's enemies? Now that is strange!'

She held him, and he liked the feel of her, warm and close and softly breathing. A languorousness stole over them both.

118

'I do not speak of your Mithras! He is a god of violence, and war, an iron god for iron men.'

Marcus was astonished.

'I do not understand you, girl.'

'Long ago, when my grandfather was a boy, a man came here, a man from the East, and he brought a young man with him. They came by sea in a strange ship. They were buying tin.'

'These islands are famous for tin. There is nothing strange in this.'

'The man's name was Joseph – he came from Arimathaea.'

'I know it.'

'They came in a ship of Tarshish and they came to the Summer Land—'

'You call this wilderness of snow the Summer Land?'

'Some there were who called it Paradise.'

'Hmph,' said Marcus, and he held her closer, only half-listening, realizing that he wanted her again. The blood had been caught on the blanket and had been turned to the outside. She would enjoy it better this time even than before.

'This Joseph was the uncle of the boy's mother, and she was called Mary—'

'And you—?'

'Yes, that is why I was given the name Mary.'

'What has all this to do with us? Your grandfather's time, you said?'

'Yes. Later Joseph had to fly from Judaea again, and he came back here, to his little house, and he built a basilica of wattle and daub. It is a most holy place.'

'More Druidic superstition, and blood sacrifices, and—'

'No! That is the point! The wine and the bread are the blood and the body of the Saviour! Not like the bull's blood—'

'What do you know of the Blood of the Bull, girl?'

He spoke more roughly than he intended, for these were high and serious matters. Gwenhwyvar shrank a little and he pulled her to him, kissing her ear, fondling her breast. 'Nay, girl, I would not betray you.'

'Yet many and many of our people have been killed – killed most horribly—'

'Your people?'

'Aye! For the young man was the Saviour, was that same Jesus Christ I serve with all my heart. And although we have been persecuted, and many slain, yet will we never relinquish our love for the living Christ!'

'By Mithras! A damned Nazarene! A serpent, in my bed!'

'Do I look like a serpent – master?'

'No! I don't give a damn if you were a Druid's witch-woman herself!' He rolled on her and grasped her, nuzzling. 'For this will endure when the world ends!'

She cried out, a low, joyful cry, as he began, and she did enjoy herself, to her eternal shame. But Gwenhwyvar, named for the Virgin Mary, promised herself that in God's good time she would save this Roman who was half a Briton like herself and so make sure his path into the everlasting paradise, that she would save his immortal soul.

The next morning before they rode out Marcus bought from the people of the village a warm sheepskin, the fleece combed and clean and finely long, and a great cloak. He paid with the bronze from his purse.

The Spanish decurion made a face.

'Why do you pay them, sir? A Roman may take what he pleases.'

Patiently, Marcus said: 'These are not enemies, decurion. One day, all in Rome's good time, they will be citizens.'

'Let them serve their twenty-five years first.'

The decurion hoicked his horse around, and kicked in his heels. Marcus stared after him. Power was for use, not abuse.

With Gwenhwyvar called Mary warmly clad and mounted on her ass they started off. An hour or so later the rear marker called that the mysterious horsemen were following up their back trail. Marcus yelled back for the decurion to do as he wished and the Spaniard hallooed and with six of his men went plunging and floundering through the snow, savagely happy to have someone against whom he might vent the frustrated fury boiling in him.

The landscape lay white-covered, the trees dripping with ice, and the snow blustering and billowing. Marcus turned to watch. The Spaniards drove their horses hard; the horsemen in the distance halted, hovered for a moment and then turned tail. They vanished into the driving snow.

Marcus bellowed for the decurion to return. He did so with a bad grace, his horse smothered with snow; but some of the violence in him had been released, and they rode on in better heart than before.

Marcus would not take the route by way of Glevum but crossed the river earlier, the water grey and icy, the snow level and cutting, very concerned over the welfare of the horses in the clumsy flat-bottomed ferry. The crossing of the Sabrina went off without a hitch except that one cavalryman smashed a hand when his horse panicked and crushed down on him. The hand was bound up and would be seen to when they reached the main camp.

With winter now ravaging the countryside, Marcus expected the Romans to take to their quarters for the season and await the coming of spring before beginning a new offensive. Frontinus was a man in a hurry, like any Roman, but he must wait on the state of the weather, like any mortal man.

In this Marcus was deceived.

Frontinus welcomed him in with the necessary civility. A little punctilious, a little absent-minded, clearly thinking of the massive preparations necessary for the days ahead. The army in their pronged attack up the valleys to the north had caught the Silures by surprise. The natives had clearly expected an attack to come in from the east. Now with the Roman system, so clear, so beautifully simple, like a fine-honed sword-blade, in action, the Silures were being driven from their richest pastures, sent packing from the lush valleys to starve on their mountain tops. Forts being built would ensure that the Silures would not return, except as slaves, in death or as subjects.

Marcus could get no word of the remaining two men he had sworn to kill to see that justice was done. Metellus Curtius and Suetonius Posthumus were actively serving, and remained for the moment outside the orbit of the governor's equerry and aide. All this time Marcus pleasured himself with Gwenhwyvar, who more and more abandoned herself to the delights of love. She had never suspected the depths of passion within herself. She gave herself willingly, joyously, responding with a fierce passion that lifted Marcus to heights of lust and abandonment to the joys of the flesh. For her part, Gwenhwyvar had vowed that despite himself she would save this Roman, in whom she saw so much of good mingled with the evil, and gloried in the knowledge that her Saviour would reserve a place at His table for Marcus Britannicus.

The often critical looks backward that occupied Marcus at

this time brought with them a calm and placid acceptance that what he had done was good. He did not gloat. He could remember Priscus, white and rigid with awful terror, trapped beneath the falling block within the cave called Wocov. He could recall the last wild plunge of Severus's horse over the sharp edge of the gorge, the splashing crunch of the body on to the rocks. And he could look back calmly to the gruesome ends of Salvius and Paulinus. No, he did not gloat. Rather, his calmness held the still final quality of the pool above the waterfall, where the river runs long and deep and powerfully before the drop. When he looked forward, to his destined meetings with Curtius and Suetonius Postumus, then it was as though the river plunged yelling over the brink, roaring and raging in a scalding foam of white water, boiling and bubbling with unleashed fury.

During these moments at night, after one of many passionate embraces, Gwenhwyvar would hold him closely, feeling the fine trembling in his limbs, hold him and soothe him, caressing, so that very soon he was ready for a fresh bout.

The weakness of his conduct depressed him. Instead of philandering his time away with the lusciousness of this girl, so newly aroused to the pleasures of love, so abandoned in her lusts, willing to copy and learn all he could teach her, he should be up and away seeking the lives of the murderer-rapists.

The winter saw campaigning enough. The Romans could not afford to allow the Silures to rest. Always they must prod and chivvy, herding them more and more away from the land that alone could give them sustenance.

So that when Frontinus summoned Marcus and, curtly, gave him his orders to scout a Silurian camp in the back hills, snow covered, bleak and bare, Marcus both welcomed and cursed the change in his life. He welcomed the opportunity to be up and doing. He cursed that he would have to tear himself away from the white blaze of passion, the lasciviousness, the sheer passion of Gwenhwyvar.

Up through the chain of forts Marcus rode, this time with two turmae of cavalry, a full sixty swords. At the last moment with the baggage and the supplies they were pushing through, he took Gwenhwyvar mounted on her ass. Her cheeks flamed rose in the chill air, and she rode with an erect back and her head held proudly. She had refused all the jewellery he would have pressed on her.

'No, my master. I have the only ornament I need.'

He laughed, thinking she referred to her own beauty. But when he expressed the thought, she flamed out at him: 'Aye, Roman! I know my breasts and my hair and my thighs and all the things that make me a woman are pleasing in men's eyes. But I care nothing for them—'

'No, by Mithras? Well, wench, I do, so take care of them!'

'This is all I care about!' And she had lifted the little object on its string about her neck. Marcus peered down.

'A worthless bauble,' he said, and even as he spoke so his hand went instinctively to the worthless pebble Boudicca had given the small boy so many years ago, the useless pebble he wore always around his neck.

Gwenhwyvar's bauble was a mere figure stamped from brass, a sign like unto a couple of greek letters intertwined, crudely done and rough as the finish indicated. She kept it always highly polished.

'What does it mean, girl?'

'That you will find out when you see the Light.'

There had been no time to argue with her, not when her young body glowed in the lamplight, white and rosy, her breasts trembling with the brass winking between them, and he had laughed and seized her up to him. Her nipples had hardened at once and the brass symbol lay forgotten between beauty. Still, now, as they rode into the interior, Marcus wondered what sign a Nazarene would put such store by, and puzzled to remember what the cynics had been saying about the evil cult back in Rome.

He had long since ceased to marvel that a cult so evil could seduce so gorgeous an innocent young girl into its black ranks. Gwenhwyvar, called Mary, with her pagan beliefs meant just one thing to him at this time; and he made very sure he took as much as he could, for the morrow no man could read.

The last fort perched on a spit of rock, a tongue protruding into the valley. Against the leaden sky the hills rose, bleak and comfortless, snow-covered, bare and forlorn.

'And that's where you'll be going this night, Britannicus.'

The fort commander, a leather-faced, gladius-backed legionary with the phalerae thick upon his breastplate nodded upwards. He'd seen it all, this senior centurion, seen it all and cared for the life of a foppish young military aide only for the advice he could bring back. The legion had been the only life, and in the legion he would serve until he could take the farm they'd give him when he retired, or until he was laid to rest, his guts chopped away by a barbarian spear. Ah, well, the world was wide and Rome bestrode the world . . .

'I'll go alone,' said Marcus, briskly. 'And I'll need Silurian clothes.'

'We have those. Aye, there have been corpses and to spare.'

So it was that night Marcus slipped out on a broken-down nag, clad in the chequered trousers and enveloping British cloak, his beard allowed to grow, his weapons those of a savage, and jog-trotted along the narrow trail up into the hills.

NINE

Just how it happened both appalled and infuriated Marcus.

Here he had been, comfortably ensconced in the Silurian mountain camp, accepted as a warrior come to join the great struggle against the hated men of iron. He had been meticulously recording in his memory all the details it was needful to know; the number of men, the number of women, the weapons, the food supplies, the layout of the fort, the state of the walls and the places of easiest access, how the sentries were posted and their efficiency and state of alertness.

Everything had been going well. This work was what he had come to Britain to do.

And then – and then a parcel of damned Druids had turned up and been treated with tremendous reverence by the savages, given to eat and drink, found places around the fires, spoken to with enormous respect. They appeared a wild and savage band of men and women in their black cloaks, carrying oaken staves with the parasite mistletoe wrapped thickly about the wood. They had intoned their ritual sayings, and having given judgment in cases of law and justice brought before them, were on the point of retiring for the night.

Then – then one of them had spoken to four hefty-looking barbarians, spoken in quiet tones, and the four had approached Marcus, and with a sword to his throat and another to his belly, the Roman had been led forward into the light from the fires.

'The beard does not hide your treachery, Roman,' said Pwyllelni, in his accented Greek. He looked very much as he had looked when Marcus had spared him and the witch-woman when they had hidden under the bank and the horsemen searched for them. But all the exhaustion was gone. The grey beard flowed as luxuriantly, and the eyes showed the fey wildness of the true fanatic. He stamped his oaken stave upon the ground so that the mistletoe wrapped about it shook and the leaves shirred with menace.

Marcus swallowed.

'I spared your life, Pwyllelni – you and the woman Rona. I

see she is here, and the babe. Would you betray me to a sure death?'

Pwyllelni, for answer, lifted up his voice.

'Listen to me, men of the hills, the painted ones, cowering in the snow. This man is a Roman, one of the men of iron, one of those who have burned and slain and raped!' He spoke in a deep belltone, chanting, the holy fires of passion burning like hell fire within him. 'What is it meet should be done to such a one?'

'Death!' they screeched, jumping up, waving their weapons, bursting into a tumult of savagery. 'Death!'

So that was to be the way of it, then . . .

A frenzied scene of shrieking and yelling, with spears and swords glinting in the firelight, of shields shaken and drummed so that the hills rang with the echoes, of men and women threatening to rush forward there and then and destroy Marcus by tearing him into a thousand tiny pieces – all this he saw and he stood, as tall and firmly as he could, feeling the sudden dryness in his mouth, the pangs of despair that there would be three bastards walking this earth when he lay mouldering beneath the sod. What could these people care for his problems, for his vows? To them he was an enemy, one who had destroyed their ancient ways. He knew how his mother's people felt. He could share much of the surface of that feeling, even if he could understand the deep currents impelling the civilization of Rome onwards.

'This is the way you requite me, then, Pwyllelni!'

'Aye, Roman cur-dog! You are weak. You held me in the palm of your hand and you did not have the courage.'

'You have no conception of mercy?'

'Mercy is for the weak.'

Then the warriors caught him and stripped him and hustled him into a hut to wait for the morning and the rituals. They would be bending the withies now, forming them into the blasphemous shape of one of their gods, a grotesque animal shape into which he would be stuffed and so burned alive. Or they would fashion one of the pools of water, smashing the ice crusting the surface, make it into a sacrificial pool and so ritually drown him. To each god the way of death of the sacrifice.

A Druidic slave chain was brought, heavy iron links, thick and clumsy but strong, and they fastened the iron loops about him, one to the throat, one to each wrist, one to each ankle.

They laughed as they did this, shrill cackling laughter that chilled the blood. And they promised what would happen to him, a catalogue of horrors that lost all meaning the longer it went on. Until he understood that what they said they meant and would do . . .

The long-drawn howling of the wolves from the hills was no more chill and hollow than the spirit within him then.

He lay on the dirt of the hut, blue with cold, shaking with ague. The chains rattled. There was a guard posted outside, who looked in every now and then, and Marcus forced himself to debate the best time to wrap his chains about the fellow's throat and choke him and so begin the escape he must essay. Thinking was not easy. The cold bit into him, the iron chafed, his head spun and he must have drifted into dream worlds of fantasy for although the night remained as dark as the breath of wind, soughing and sending snow flurries in through the open door, told him that the weak and pallid dawn could not be far off. Now, then, must be the time.

The howling of the wolves had grown. They had sounded far and distant all the time he had ridden here, and they had been completely forgotten when he had been scouting the camp. But now their wild ululations, reminding him of the hunting dogs he had used to such good purpose, closed around the hill camp. He heard the guard muttering, and an answering voice, and as the guards changed he caught their blasphemous opinions of the wolves forever infesting the hills.

Presently, feeling as stiff as blood-soaked leather left over-night on a corpse, he roused himself and stood up. The lowness of the hut's roof forced him to crouch. He had to move with exquisite caution lest the iron links jangled and so betrayed him. He took his position beside the door, and held his arms in the best position, and so waited.

The guard hawked and spat and shifted his stance. His iron-shod spear butt scraped the frozen ground. The wolves were now so close their noise forced itself upon Marcus's attention. He heard a distant shouting, thin and scattered, and the little breeze wafted the sounds away, only to slacken and let them return, louder.

Abruptly the shouting burst up, drowning the sough of the breeze. The guard shouted. Marcus knew that the time had come.

Carefully, he inched into the open doorway with the cloth

thrown back. He looked out. The guard stood with his back to him, peering down the street in the grey wanness of that illusory period of lightness before true dawn. Marcus wrapped the chains about his neck, dragged them tight and heaved back. The guard's neck cracked like a broken pitcher.

The body tumbled into the dirt as Marcus released him and stepped back.

People were running among the huts. Some ran towards the walls, others away, into the huts. Men with weapons raced by, not looking at him. He heard now, above the shouting, the ferocious blood-crazed shrieking of wolves. Wolves! The symbol of Rome! Wolves, here, raging into the camp, long low lean grey shapes, running with lolling tongues and fiery eyes, racing between the huts. A woman fell and wolves clustered about her, bristling, ferocious, their hunger giving them fangs of iron.

The chains would be an encumbrance. No one seemed to care about him. The dead guard's dagger broke as Marcus tried to lever and force the iron links apart. He threw the thing away, and all the time kept a watchful eye open should a wolf prowl his way. The uproar in the camp racketted on. Men were slashing at the wolves, and more and more of the vulpine shapes poured into the camp, coming up from the direction of the main entrance. This oppidan, built on the usual British ideas of a hill fort, seemed full of wolves.

A group of men rushed along between the huts, their weapons pale bars of blue-white steel in the treacherous light. Marcus hunkered down, in the shadows. The men raced past. Then – he did not believe it. He stared, and still did not believe.

'Britannicus! Master – you are alive! I give thanks to the Saviour!'

'Gwenhwyvar! Now, by Mithras, wench – what—?'

'Do not waste time – master! Come – Come quickly. There are horses here – but hurry, hurry!'

She wore her cloak enveloped around her and as she reached out a hand to pull him up the cloak fell apart. The upper part of her body was nude. Four richly red prints showed upon her waist, beneath her left breast. As she drew the cloak together Marcus noticed how red the nipple was, how scarlet and hard and proud it was. Her face flamed. 'Hurry!'

'So that is how you got in. But – but the wolves?'

128

She lifted her left arm. A cut showed from which the blood no longer flowed, gathered into a clot about the wound. 'I cut myself and dropped the blood down, and they followed. I did not fear for myself; but I feared lest they catch me before I reached the camp.'

The horses were rapidly untied from the back of the next hut. A wolf slowly stalked forward from the shadows and the girl checked her instinctive scream. Despite the jangling chains Marcus could still grip the dead guard's sword. He set himself. The wolf, its red eyes smoky in the erratic light, had lost all fear of men with the pains of hunger in its belly. It hurled itself forward. The blade came around with a meaty chunk and as Marcus leaped aside the wolf flopped to the ground, cut open, rich blood pouring out to smoke upon the ground.

'Up, girl!'

'You first – the chains—'

Somehow they mounted up, Marcus with his legs cocked up with the chain taut between them. They led out. More wolves passed and the horses whinnied and then broke into clumsy gallops as Gwenhwyvar hit them both, first Marcus's and then hers. They galloped at breakneck speed between the huts and as they neared the opening in the oppidan walls of ramped earth so that last period of darkness before dawn closed down. Commending himself to Mithras, Marcus allowed the horse to make his own way.

Together, side by side, they thundered over the frozen ground, out past the first ditch, past the second, galloping over the ramp to freedom. Three warriors appeared like ghosts before them and Marcus managed to let his instincts ride out the crisis. Head down he yelled: 'Wolves! Wolves everywhere! Ride for your lives!'

The three scurried like frightened conies.

They were out past the last ditch, out on to the open frigid ground. The darkness held for them. Each praised a different god, but each gave thanks as their horses sure-footedly took them down the hill and away. Behind them the frenzied howling of the wolves slackened as grey muzzles buried in soft intestines and as the Silures crept up, sword in hand, to finish off the wolves, every last one.

'And you say this slave wench cut herself and used her blood to draw the wolves? And seduced a guard to open the gate to let her in—'

'Aye, and when he was occupied and the gate open the wolves came through. Do you wonder I wish for manumission for her?'

The senior centurion sniffed. Pretty soon all the world would have the precious gift of Roman citizenship, and then there would be no value in it, for there would be no one without it.

'I'd suggest you carried out the necessary formalities when you get back to the fort. It will be better there, and more legal.'

Marcus laughed. He felt wonderful. Gwenhwyvar would be all right, as would he. Riding naked through the snow was not something he would relish; but it had had its moments. Now he could get back to Frontinus and then he would free Gwenhwyvar.

So they rode back, with their escort, warmly clad. And Marcus did all that was necessary in the prescribed way and Gwenhwyvar knelt at his feet at the crossroads and he lifted her up and said: 'You are free to take what road you wish.'

And she looked up at him, and smiled, and said: 'I will stay with you – master.'

The prospect warmed his loins, no doubt of it.

'You need never call me master again. You have told me that you serve only one Master.'

'That is true. Yet—'

'And did this Nazarene of yours really come to this land of mist in the long ago?'

'I have told you. My grandfather saw Him. And, also, he helped to build the basilica for Joseph, on the island. It is a most sacred place—'

'Full of oak groves and mistletoe—'

'No!' she flamed at him. 'A little wattle and daub church, that my grandfather helped to build, on the island, and Joseph taught us of Him—'

'And you will never teach me of your Nazarene, my Gwenhwyvar!'

Then the witnessess crowded forward, congratulating them both, and the deed was done and seen to be done, with the legalities of the manumission written out fair for all to see.

Frontinus expressed himself well-pleased with Marcus's work.

'They ran like conies when the caligatae got in amongst 'em. By the Emperor and all his family! We shall finish this campaign with the help of winter – then it will be the turn of the Ordovices.'

During the rest of that winter living in comfortable quarters, called only rarely for arduous duties and these soon over, Marcus led a most wonderful life. The passion between him and Gwenhwyvar flared into the most abandoned lust. Nothing was impossible. Marcus did not know and did not care if they truly loved each other. The only thing that mattered was the pure pleasure of their love-making. Mary's body held an allure he could not resist. Time after time he would groan and roll back and shake his head and – a few cupfuls of wine later she would reach for him and caress him and arouse him and again he would plunge into joyous debauchery. They were both insatiable. And, all the time, insidiously, this Mary worked on Marcus to bring him to her way of thinking. She told him much of the inner lore of her beliefs, of the teachings of this Nazarene, this Jesus Christ, and showed him that the brass bauble that dangled between beauty was a symbol in some foreign written tongue for the letters of His name.

'And forgiveness of our enemies, Marcus, my love! That is what He said. He said you must turn the other cheek if you are struck—'

'You mean stand off so as to get a better swing at the fellow?'

'No, no, my love.' She sighed. 'If a man hits you you must turn the other cheek, so as to let him hit you again—'

'By Mithras! That old rogue Pwyllelni said this Nazarene would lead everyone to slavery, and the old devil was right!'

'There is no slavery save of the body, Marcus! In Paradise we shall sit on His right hand, in splendour – Vengeance is mine, that is what He said—'

'My mother—'

'Hush, my dear. It saddens me – and you frighten me. That man in the Wocov – he was evil, yes; but it is not given to mortal men to take revenge—'

'I do not seek revenge! Revenge is for the mean-spirited. I seek for justice.'

So they wrangled, and slowly Marcus gave in, bit by bit, as Gwenhwyvar worked on him, her sensuousness overpowering the vengeance within him, her beauty driving everything else from his heart.

So much passion they shared, so much sheer lust for love lay between them, that they feared they would consume all in the very fierceness of their love. But the more they made love the more they demanded, relishing every moment, never sated, always living for the glance of the other's eyes, the touch of a hand, the arousing of desire, the beginning in voluptuous infatuation the culmination in perfect peace – until the next time.

Her body drove Marcus frantic with desire. Voluptuous, sensuous, curved and smooth and beating with the warm pink pulse of blood beneath the smooth whiteness of skin – the smell and sight of her could send him rigid and fiercely demanding at any hour. Often and often they would have to excuse themselves from a dinner in the triclinium and retire to a private room to assuage themselves of the lust burning like molten gold through every fibre of their bodies. Joined in mutual ecstasy they would ride the storm of passion and slowly recover themselves and realize they but inhabited a mortal world, and so, tidying their hair and clothes, return to smile and talk and laugh with the guests.

All this through the spring and early summer – until the day Frontinus, sending for Marcus, shattered the bubble of illusion.

Thinking this merely a routine chore, dull and of no importance, Marcus fisted his breast and waited.

'Ah, Britannicus. Just the man.' Frontinus, as always, very busy with his maps and lists and messages. 'I hear great things of this little girl you have – a nice thing – now, to business. The Ninth are at it again, and they need a scout.'

The Ninth! The Second Augusta here in the south and the Twentieth Valeria Victrix from further north at Vriconium were fully engaged with finishing the Silures and penetrating into the Ordovician strongholds. The Second Adiutrix with the brand new quarters at Deva enlarged from the old fort there would also have their work cut out. So it had been left to the Ninth Hispana from their headquarters at Eboracum to keep an eye on a vast territory. Vexillations from this legion, as Marcus knew, had reduced its strength. Now, these detachments were returned to the parent unit as the Second Adiutrix came into the line.

'The Britons cut up an auxiliary cohort with their damned chariots, Britannicus. You will have to make all speed to the east – the country there is superb for chariot-fighting – and report in to Fronto and then act under his orders. The Ninth is a tough outfit. I want this festering spot cleared up quickly.'

Marcus could understand that. Frontinus was engaged on what could turn out to be the last campaign in the west, for with the Cornovii and the Deceangli already pacified and the war going well against the Ordovices, there would remain only the Gangani, a small tribe in a narrow peninsula, and the Demetae to deal with. After that – well, men spoke of reports of another island to the west, a land of savagery and evil and altogether far more unpleasant than Britain. Marcus rather fancied that his work here in the land of mist would be done before then, and he would be on the road south of Rome, heading for Pompeii.

So that, whilst the governor bent every effort here in the west he wanted no trouble spots in his rear. They must be expunged, quickly, ruthlessly and finally.

The battle had been brief and bitter and bloody.

The Celtic chariots had whirled on, dust spouting from their wheels and the horses' hooves, their harness jingling, the sun glinting back in silver and golden reflections. The horses' heads, upreared against the sunlight, the wild warriors with streaming hair and painted bodies, screeching their war-cries, had impressed the old foot-sloggers of the Ninth not one whit. The Roman auxiliary cavalry had darted in, like stinging insects on the flanks of crazed cattle; their javelins had created the first havoc.

The auxiliary infantry had broken. The chariots in clouds of riven dust whirled on – and crashed headlong into the iron wall of the legion.

Warrior after warrior pitched from the swaying cars as the pila pierced them through. The hastati men stepped forward and drove their massive spears upwards, solid thunking blows that smashed through flimsy armour – or through flesh and bone where the savage barbarians disdained altogether the use of armour and rode screaming into battle all bare and painted.

The square cylindrical shields of the legion locked. The swords licked out as the horses screamed and reared and spun away. The noise and confusion and dust and horror lay all within the broken charioteers; the men of the legion went methodically forward, a battering roller of sheer power.

The Roman cavalry would not let the chariots be. Streaming lines of men pressed close to their horses' necks swerved in to hurl their javelins and then spin away, easily eluding the clumsy dashes of the chariots. Wheels buckled and broke under the strain and men were pitched out under the iron hooves.

Through the whole action the glittering Eagle of the Ninth surrounded by the First Cohort seemed to shower sparks of golden light upon the ranks of the legion. Men could see the Eagle and feel uplifted and know that the iron will of Rome would never be checked.

Riding on hard and not caring if he left his cavalry escort and Gwenhwyvar and the baggage far behind Marcus lashed his horse on. By Mithras! Ahead lay the dust and boil of a battle, with the Legion solidly earning their salt, and here he was, flogging on a tired horse and about to come up to the action when it would all be over! He thirsted to get into the fight. The escort plunged along after him, mere specks out of the corners of his eyes.

He jumped a smashed chariot and saw the driver with a pilum through his throat and the fighting-man at his side, his head crushed.

Now he was up with the turmoil and for a few crazed moments could lay about him joyfully, venting all the spite he felt at a long exhausting ride ending in anticlimax.

The battle was over.

Wrecked chariots lay scattered over the plain like heaps of firewood. Horses screamed and galloped wildly, in every direction. Men sprawled in death, and others heaved up their guts, and others simply lay and shrieked. The Legion hardly needed to dress and re-form ranks, so complete had been their discipline.

Hard, were the men of the Legions, hard and with a devout and complete belief in the invincibility of their Eagles.

Gwenhwyvar caught up with Marcus as he trotted into a narrow gulley leading to a defile that, eventually, trended away off the plain into the ever-present woodlands. He was scarcely conscious of her. Ahead rode three Celts, all wounded, all riding wounded horses, a pitiful remainder of the armed might that had ridden out earlier with their chariots.

What fate drove Marcus on he might never fully understand; he knew only that virtue and fate interlinked to give him the powerful help of Mithras. He caught the three and there was no difficulty in despatching them; for their spirit had been broken as their fighting strength had been shattered. It had been like this when his great aunt Boudicca had seen her army routed.

He halted his horse and breathed in deeply. The shadows of evening were beginning to fall and he wanted now to return to the legionary camp and take a bath and refresh himself. He saw Gwenhwyvar trotting after him, into a widening space in the gulley. Rough stones carpeted the track and the horses trod carefully. He heard a horse whinny ahead.

'For the sake of Mithras! Here! Help me!'

The shout whispered weakly from a group of four horses ahead. They stood as though picketted. To this spot the three Celts had been riding. Intrigued, Marcus urged his horse over and so came to rest looking down on the naked man, staked out, blood covering his body and face from the many small wounds inflicted on him. He was clearly in great pain. His heavy head rolled from side to side, the shorn Roman hairstyle glistened with sweat.

'You poor devil,' said Marcus. He dismounted at once and drew his pugio. 'Hold still whilst I cut you free, friend.'

To each wrist and each ankle a rope had been fastened. The other ends of the ropes had been tied each to a horse's harness. A fifth rope had been wound in such a way that it secured the horses to the stakes. A single slash would free them. A cut across their rumps would send them off in four different directions. As they ran so each would haul an arm or a leg. The man would burst asunder.

'They caught me,' the man whispered. His blood-smothered face reflected the horrors he had gone through. 'They – they—' He licked his lips. Gwenhwyvar appeared at Marcus's side with a water-bottle. The liquid dropped upon the man's face, and he licked greedily, like an exhausted dog after a chase.

'We'll soon have you out of this,' said Marcus. 'It will need care to cut the right ropes.'

'I thank you—'

'Why thank me? This is only what any Roman would do for another. I am Marcus Julius Britannicus. Now, hold steady—'

'Yet do I thank you for rescuing me – I am Lucius Metellus Curtius—'

The dagger in Marcus's hand kissed a rope holding a wrist. It poised, unmoving save for a fine tremble that shot a ripple of light from the honed blade.

'Metellus Curtius?'

'Yes. Tribune with the Ninth—'

'I see,' said Marcus, and he sat back on his heels.

'Why do you hesitate, Marcus?' demanded Gwenhwyvar. She took out her own little knife with the ivory hilt given her by Marcus and she knelt to the man's bonds.

'Soft, my love,' said Marcus. Then: 'I think it meet you should go back to the horses. I would not wish them to stray.'

Gwenhwyvar, who was called Mary, understood.

'This man – this Metellus Curtius, is one of—'

'Yes.'

She turned to Marcus, her face radiant, her eyes devouring him with the inner fire, the spirit that irradiated her.

'Why then, Marcus, my love! Now is your chance! Now is the God-given opportunity for you to prove your manhood, your brotherhood in Christ! Long have I prayed for the opportunity!'

'And long have I prayed for this moment, Gwenhwyvar.'

'What—?' said Metellus Curtius. He tried to twist up to look at them, and the pain flowed over him, and he cried out and fell back.

'Go back to the horses, Gwenhwyvar.'

'But Marcus! You cannot kill this man. Not now, not after what you know is the true way! I have explained to you – many and many a time – vengeance belongs to God – it is not for a mere man—'

'You do not make sense, Gwenhwyvar.' The dagger trembled. 'You know what this piece of offal did to my mother? How can you say manhood demands I forgive him? Forgiveness must be earned. And this whoreson might begin learning by dying.'

Metellus Curtius struggled against the ropes, and through his pain he cried out. 'What are you talking about? Cut me free, Britannicus. Cut me free for the sake of the Eagle!'

'For the sake of the Eagle you must die, Curtius.'

'Die! But you have rescued me! What nonsense is this?'

'I will tell you, Metellus Curtius, tell you of a certain merry party held by the officers of the Ninth – some of them, that is – and of a Princess of the Iceni and of a treasure, and of rape and torture and murder.'

Before he had gone far in his quiet talking, Marcus stopped as Curtius, sweating now so that the drops mingled and blended with the blood upon him, cried out woefully: 'Yes, yes! I was there! But it was not me who put the hot irons to her! I did not cut her!'

The veins stood out on Marcus's forehead. He leaned down and struck Curtius across the face, so that the man's head jumped sideways, and he screamed.

'You whoreson spawn! You bastard! You raped and tortured and killed, and now you will suffer more than these poor fools of Celts know how to make you suffer!'

'Please, Marcus!' Gwenhwyvar trembled, her face white, her hands gripped before her and pressed against her as she knelt. 'I beg you, Marcus, for the sake of your immortal soul! You cannot bring back your poor mother by this – and you will lose much—'

'I have lost everything already, so I do not care a brass quadrans!'

Curtius screamed again, straining through his pain at the ropes binding him.

'I did not! I did not! It was Condorus who told us of the treasure – he suggested it all! Not me! I only did what the others did, across the table. But Vellius Condorus told us of the treasure of the Iceni bitch, said it was ours by rights, said he would make her talk—'

A great many things suddenly made sense to Marcus. He felt a coldness in his stomach, a coldness at the back of his neck. He shook so that the dagger stuttered in shards of silver fire above the bound and helpless man.

'Vellius Condorus!'

No need now to ask who had sent those assassins to slay him in Aquae Sulis. A procurator had been seen by Frontinus that evening; but Marcus had been too anxious to hare off to the brothel to pay attention. And he had talked with Condorus. No wonder horsemen had followed. The snow and the cold had foiled them then, they and the vigorous inspection of the Spanish decurion. So now there was another name to add to the list. There remained Suetonius Postumus and Vellius Condrous and fat Crassus in Pompeii.

This one here, this Metellus Curtius, was a dead man for all the pleadings of Gwenhwyvar.

Marcus vented the terrible anger consuming him. He told Curtius what he was going to do, and Gwenhwyvar cried out and caught his arm and begged him. She pleaded and cried and besought him. They both understood this was a crisis in their relationship.

'I thought you understood, Marcus, my love! I thought I had won you over! Only a short time, I believed, and you would be one of us! We abhor violence! Vengeance is not for mortal man – oh, Marcus, my dear love, please, please – give over this vengeance!'

Marcus tried to break free from her grip and she would not let him go.

He turned and without passion, without thought, blindly, as a hunted animal seeks its burrow when the hounds bay, he struck her away. She fell, a hand to her cheek, her eyes burning. She fell back and she did not cry out. And Marcus left her and turned back to the consummation of his vengeance.

'No, Britannicus! I did but do what the others did – no! I beg you! Please, do not—'

'You did what the others did, and you will suffer as the others suffered, as the remaining three will suffer! You should not have insulted a Princess of the Iceni who was my mother. You should have taken some drab from the kitchens for your sport! But – my mother! This, I do, this I serve you as I served Paulinus and Salvius—'

Curtius screamed and then his mouth was filled and the blood ran down his chin, and Gwenhwyvar shuddered and hid her face.

'Farewell, you cur-dog, Metellus Curtius!'

And Marcus struck down with the dagger and severed the retaining rope and the horses started up and he struck them, mercilessly, and they pawed the air and galloped frenziedly away in different directions. They were checked for a moment; but only for a brief moment, and then they galloped on, and each horse trailed a bloody hunk of meat tumbling at the end of its rope.

The day was dying. It was time to return to camp.

Marcus turned to Gwenhwyvar. He felt detached, calm, cool with the knowledge of what he had done and what remained.

He felt surprise. Gwenhwyvar had mounted up, was catching the reins and bringing her horse's head around. He stepped towards his horse, holding out his hand.

'Wait for me, Mary – it is late and I need the comfort of your presence tonight – your presence and your love.'

'I have failed, Marcus – my love. I am filled with sin. I

cannot stay – and I sin if I leave, and yet I cannot stay. You are a man of iron, a man of blood.'

'Mary! What are you saying?'

'Farewell, Marcus. I am not fit to be called Mary. My Saviour suffered on a cross for me – that young man who came to my land in the long ago, of whom we were told by Joseph of Arimathaea – and I cannot suffer any longer for you.'

'I do not want you to suffer! Love – I want love—'

'You are destroying yourself, my Marcus. Vengeance will eat you away as the rain eats away the salt mountain. And I cannot live beside you and watch you—'

'There is no argument about the justice of my vengeance, Gwenhwyvar – Mary! This is Rome. No moral judgments enter into these things, no doubts, no self-questioning. These things have been done, and these things remain to be done.'

'I have failed to teach the way, to show you the Light. I suffer for you, my Marcus, and I am weak and cannot rest to see you destroy yourself. I must go, Marcus, my darling – I must! And I will pray that, one day, my Saviour will save you as I pray Him to save you – and to save me, also.'

She kicked her horse and rode away.

Stupefied, not understanding, Marcus stared after her.

She had ridden away, out of his life. He knew enough about her to know her decision might have tortured her; but she had made it and he could not sway her away from it. She had left him.

And he felt her sorrow for him and, mingled with the sorrow, a repugnance that dizzied him, that denied his manhood.

Four horses ran aimlessly, goaded by the stink of blood tumbling about after them, pursuing them, a stink they could not outrun.

TEN

'Vulpus the Fox! Reds! Reds! Zephyr!'

Other shouts smashed into the overheated air, 'Green! Blue! Eutychus! Eusebius!'

No one shrieked for White and many Whites had transferred their allegiance to Red.

The quadrigas hurled down the straight smoking dust haring for the last bend. The last dolphin, the last ball, and then the headlong hurtle down the straight to the winning line and the vociferous welcome to the victor.

The febrile excitement of the race no longer touched Marcus. He remembered that whoreson bastard Metellus Curtius being torn asunder, being dragged in four separate directions, and he drove his four in with delicate, ruthless precision, guiding Zephyr his superb funalis in with a pressure – never a blow – from the whip.

His nearside iron-rimmed wheel snicked in behind Green's. With exquisite care as the chariots careered along in headlong flight Marcus hauled out. The wheels grated. The cars plunged. With a wild smother of spraying wheels and splinters of wood Eutychus's wheel wrenched off and his car struck the sand once and flew to flinders.

The charioteer went over the rail, shrieking, the knife in his hand flailing at the ribbons. Marcus stood up, tall, let the whip flick once and then cracked it down over the backs of the four. The smashing report sent them into their last mad run. Sand kicked up, the chariot bounded high, the hooves glittered through the dust. On his right Blue howled like a maniac and lashed his horses on. Eusebius had used his whip often and to good effect; now the horses did not respond as they might have done had Eusebius reserved the punishment for the climactic moment.

Poppaea felt the young man's fingers and felt the delicious wetness and warmth of herself, the shrieking made her jaws ache and yet she could not stop screaming. He was rigid with the excitement and Poppaea clutched and clutched and the stands were a single howling mass.

Like two darts from a single ballista the chariots flew for the finish.

The words of the Dominus, of fat and evil Clodius, found a faint echo in Marcus's skull.

'If you win this race, Vulpus, you are a dead man!'

The whip flicked again and cracked with a sound of a marble block splitting asunder. The horses responded. Now Zephyr ran with unerring purity along the rail, a hair's breadth away and Blue edged in, trying to box Marcus in against the rail.

Marcus slashed his whip at Eusebius and the man flinched. His nerve gave. He shrieked an unheard oath and hauled out and Red shot through on the rail. The winning line poured up like the brink of a waterfall and Blue dropped back and the slaves were running out and the red scarf was being waved with mad abandon and the cavea sent thunderous bellows of sound high into the heated air of Imperial Rome.

And Red had won! Marcus had won!

The horses, sweat covered, lathered, gleaming and yet coated with dust, pranced and pirouetted. Slaves ran to calm them and guide them through the exit stalls.

Clodius was there. Marcus stared stonily, his face a graven mask of iron, indifferent to the fat equestrian's insane exhibition of anger – an anger at winning he must cloak with cries of pleasure. Marcus knew well enough his hired assassins would be given their orders, that Marcus would feel the dagger beneath his ribs, find a hole in the Tiber.

Deliberately, he shook the reins. The slaves clinging to the horses' heads cried out. Marcus flicked the whip down, casually. The tip stung Zephyr on the rump. Startled, the funalis lunged forward. His razor-sharp hooves lifted, pawing, his startled whinny reverberated in the exit stall.

Clodius threw up an arm in horror.

The quadriga rolled on, inexorably, and Marcus let the reins fall loose. He made no effort to haul back.

Like many a good warrior of the Iceni, like many a good charioteer of the Circus, Clodius Maximus went down under the hooves and wheels of a quadriga.

There would be a great deal of running and shouting, many inquiries, dutiful noises made by Vulpus the Fox.

But he was free of this incubus.

Vulpus the Fox would continue to fight in the amphitheatre

and to race in the Circus, and the enormous fickle crowds of Rome would continue to shout for their favourite.

And Marcus Julius Britannicus would continue to pursue the cruel destiny that marked him out from all other men in this glittering Empire of Rome.

Favourite reading from Mayflower Books
A list of established Bestsellers you may have missed